SUNRISE ISLAND SISTERS

Sunrise Island Series
Book 2

Maren Hill

The series prequel, **Cliffhouse Footprints**, is available free to my email subscribers only, for a limited time. Please see my website at www.marenhill.com or scan the QR code below:

Chapter One

Even in the dim moonlight, Kyla could tell the man ahead was striking. She had been strolling barefoot by the ocean when she spotted a bare-chested man knee-deep in the water. He didn't look familiar; perhaps he was a new resident of the ecovillage or a temporary worker. Kyla slowed, uncertain if she should keep walking or return to her room.

"Nice night for a swim, don't you think?" he asked as she approached.

"Couldn't be more perfect," Kyla replied, savouring his deep voice. She couldn't help admiring his stunning physique and how his low-cut shorts hinted at what lay beneath.

Feeling more relaxed after a few glasses of cider with her friends in the common room, Kyla waded into the ocean, her gaze fixed on the stranger, who never looked away—and she liked that. Now within reach, Jude asked if she'd like to dance. Kyla giggled, feeling as though she was on a movie set, fully immersed in whatever this crazy, fun scene might become—

until a splash of frigid ocean water sent her racing to shore, screaming.

Jude laughed as he followed. "Yeah, it's freakin' cold, I know," he said. "Why don't we go back to my place and warm up?"

Kyla chuckled at his bold approach. "I have no idea who you are," she said.

"We can fix that in two seconds," he said with a playful grin, raising his voice over the crash of waves. "I'm Jude, one of those quirky organic farmers working for room and board. Today's my last day here." He extended his hand.

Kyla looked up at him and introduced herself. "You're a member of WWOOF," she acknowledged, feeling the warmth of his large hand envelop hers in a gentle but firm shake.

As they walked closer to the ecovillage, the outdoor lights gently highlighted each other's faces.

"Oh, I'm sorry. I must have missed you somehow. I don't remember seeing you at the orientation," Kyla said, certain she would have remembered such a stunningly gorgeous man.

"I wasn't there. I was in town making travel arrangements for tomorrow," Jude explained, folding his arms across his chest. "Look, I need to get some clothes on, and I'm sure you want to dry off, Kyla."

Sensing the conversation winding down, Kyla hoped she hadn't missed her chance to get to know Jude better. She couldn't let that happen; after all, he'd have no trouble finding someone else to spend time with him.

"I'm in Room Three," Jude said, pointing toward the exchange workers' housing. "If you care to join me, I'll be ready in fifteen minutes with two glasses of chilled organic wine—one with your name on it."

"Only because it's your last night," Kyla teased, turning

toward the main building. She floated up the stairs, already planning her sexiest outfit.

In an off-the-shoulder top, matching black skirt, and strappy sandals, Kyla knocked lightly on the door of Room Three. Jude opened the door and paused, his gaze sweeping slowly from head to toe. "Hello, Beautiful," he said, guiding her inside.

Kyla hadn't been with a man in months, so she was hungry. As Jude leaned in to offer her a glass of organic Sauvignon Blanc, the attraction between them felt magnetic. It wasn't long before they were wrapped in each other's arms, exchanging endless kisses that touched the depths of Kyla's soul. Caught in the vortex of feverish lovemaking, Kyla cast aside all restraint and surrendered completely to the passion Jude ignited.

In the early morning light, alone in the room where they'd made love, Kyla found a torn piece of paper on the bedside table with a handwritten note:

I'll think about last night all day.

Chapter Two

Kyla rarely took a day off from her job at Dr. Nicholl's veterinary clinic. It wasn't just because "Mr. Grumpy Pants Supreme", as she secretly called him, would throw a fit, but also because she was saving for her dream home. She envisioned a quaint cottage nestled in the forest, perched on a cliff overlooking the ocean. Even though she fantasized about owning a waterfront getaway, she knew it was out of her financial reach at the moment. But she wasn't one to give up on her dreams.

Living in EarthSong Village was a perfect fit for Kyla. It resonated with her outgoing nature and her love of being surrounded by people. She thrived in the communal lifestyle—sharing meals, singing, dancing, hiking, kayaking, and tending to the sustainable gardens. The ecovillage buzzed with activity and camaraderie. Some members were passionate environmentalists, vigilantly monitoring issues like old-growth forest logging and organizing protests and campaigns to protect the precious environment. This sense of purpose and community made EarthSong feel like home to Kyla.

While she embraced much of the ecovillage's philosophy, she had her limits. She felt uneasy about sharing beds and what she saw as excessive marijuana use. While she never judged others for their choices, she held firm to the values instilled in her by her family. With Kathleen, her wise and nurturing grandmother, and Jennie, her strong and principled mother, how could she not? Their influence had shaped her into someone who knew where to draw the line, even in a place as free-spirited as EarthSong.

Kyla's closest friend in the ecovillage was known as Raine, a woman in her early twenties with long, wavy hair often worn in a messy braid. The faint scent of patchouli mixed with lavender was as characteristic of Raine as her worn leather sandals and flowy clothing. While Kyla went by Sundance among her friends in the ecovillage, her family steadfastly referred to her by her birth name, refusing to use any other.

Kyla and Raine had planned to spend the upcoming long weekend at a meditation retreat on Cortes Island, but their journey would be anything but straightforward. They would hitch a ride to the ferry terminal at Fulford Harbour, cross to Swartz Bay on Vancouver Island, and then catch a bus to downtown Victoria. From there, they'd continue their trek to Nanaimo and Campbell River, with the final leg involving catching another ferry ride to Gorge Harbour on Cortes Island.

After more than eleven hours of travel, they'd finally arrive at "Goldenrod," a serene oceanside retreat nestled in a dense forest with breathtaking sea views. Once there, they would unwind and settle into their cozy cabin, ready for a weekend of peace and reflection.

While waiting for the nine o'clock sailing to Swartz Bay, Kyla and Raine stood outside in the morning sun. Raine decided to check her mailbox at the postal outlet, a short walk toward the town centre.

"My brother Mark said he sent something for my birthday," Raine explained to Kyla. "I'll be right back," she called over her shoulder as she headed down the walkway toward the post office.

A few minutes later, Raine returned to Kyla with a foil-wrapped package in her hand, piquing Kyla's curiosity. "Oh," Kyla said, raising her brows, "what's in that?"

"Don't know," Raine replied with a shrug. "I took off the outside packaging and found another wrapped package inside."

"Ha!" Kyla chuckled. "It looks like a loaf of tea bread or something. Is your brother a baker?"

Raine laughed. "Not at all. He works on a farm near Tillamook, Oregon. He gets room and board in exchange for his work and lives in a wood-frame house on the edge of a hundred-acre farm."

"Sweet," Kyla said, eyeing the package. "Are you planning to keep it wrapped for your birthday, or will you open it at the cabin?"

"You know," Raine said thoughtfully, "Mark mentioned it needs refrigeration. I'm not quite sure what to do with it yet, but yes, I'm planning to save it for my real birthday on Monday."

Kyla furrowed her brows, lost in thought, her lips pursed and eyes narrowing as she considered her friend's plight.

"If you want," Kyla suggested, "you could store it in my sister Alexa's fridge. I have a key, and I'm sure she wouldn't mind."

Kyla watched as Raine checked her phone. "We have plenty of time to get to Grace Square before the ferry arrives," Raine said. "Aren't we smart for getting here early?"

Kyla laughed. "What's the expression? Something about living on 'Sunrise Island time', like we have a schedule exclusive to residents."

"Yep," Raine grinned. "And I hear there are real hippies on Sunrise Island." She chuckled. "I love your idea, Sundance. Let's stash this baby in your sister's fridge."

To make sure everything was set, Kyla added, "I'll text her and let her know not to touch it."

* * *

In Alexa's apartment, Kyla reconsidered. "Better put it in the freezer since we'll be off-island for four days." She opened the small compartment above the fridge, which was empty except for a carton of ice cubes.

"My sister buys things fresh and doesn't eat meat, so your brother's gift has the freezer all to itself," Kyla said as Raine placed the package on the bottom shelf and closed the door.

"Perfect," Raine said. "Nice apartment your sister has. It's so organized and clean—different from our place, huh, Sundance?"

"Quite," Kyla replied. "My sister and I are different in many ways, but similar in others. I love her, but we don't hang out as often as I'd like."

Kyla locked the door, and they walked down two flights of stairs. As they headed back to the ferry terminal, their conversation continued.

"Yeah, with both of you working and the busy schedules at EarthSong, I can see why you don't have much time to spend with your sister," Raine said.

"Plus, we hang with different crowds," Kyla added. "You haven't even met Alexa, and you've lived here all your life. And she's my sister."

"True," Raine agreed. "We say 'everyone knows everyone' here, but that's not one hundred percent accurate."

"I have to admit," Kyla said with a chuckle, "some people

don't want us around. They call us 'hippies' and think we don't bathe."

"Yep," Raine said knowingly. "Free love, drugged-out minds—livin' off the land—since when is that crime?"

As the ferry approached, they quickened their pace and joined the boarding line.

* * *

Exhausted after the long journey, Kyla and Raine retrieved the key to their cabin from the reception desk. It was in an envelope marked with Kyla's name, along with a boxed meal.

"I'm famished," Kyla remarked, pleased that the retreat organizers had thoughtfully left dinner for them, given their late arrival.

Following a well-lit wood-chip path to Cabin #6, they eagerly devoured their meals and settled in for the night.

Chapter Three

In her apartment in Grace Square, Alexa was jolted awake by a throbbing headache that pulled her from a deep sleep. She noticed a dull ache in her right wrist, but it was overshadowed by the raw scrapes and sensitive bruises scattered across her body, in areas not shielded from the fall by her thick robe.

Still feeling disoriented, Alexa glanced at the clock on her bedside table and her heart sank. She was late for work. Although she had no intention of going in today, she should have called Dr. Cindy. Being late for work was one thing, Alexa chided herself, but failing to explain was another matter entirely.

A new wave of apprehension washed over Alexa. What would she say to Dr. Cindy? That her sister had left her drugged out of her mind, so she couldn't come in today?

Despite her woes, Alexa found herself laughing out loud in her apartment. *Sometimes you have to laugh,* she thought, *it's either that or cry.* She picked up the phone at 9:00 a.m., a half-hour past the clinic's opening. She could picture Dr. Cindy juggling both treatment rooms, a waiting room full of patients, and no one at the front desk.

"Dr. Cindy," Alexa began, leaving her message, "I'm so sorry for not calling sooner. I had an unfortunate accident last night and was knocked unconscious." She hoped mentioning being 'unconscious' might earn her some leniency. "I just woke up five minutes ago and couldn't call earlier. I know this is a terrible inconvenience, but I'll be in on Monday. Please don't worry."

Alexa managed to finish her entire message before the beep. She hoped Dr. Cindy would understand why no one had called on her behalf, knowing she lived alone. Until today, Alexa had never missed a day of work—*just another fallout from the accident,* she thought bitterly.

* * *

As Alexa ended the call, relieved to have left her message, her voicemail pinged with a new message. She listened, and Dr. Cindy's voice came through:

Hi Alexa, this is Cindy. I don't know why you're not at work today, but please give me a call as soon as you can. You know it's New Patient Day, and it's not the best time to be absent.

Alexa sighed, realizing that Cindy had called before she could send her own message. She felt a stab of regret at the thought of disrupting New Patient Day, knowing how crucial it was for the clinic.

Chapter Four

Alexa's mission for the weekend was clear: get well enough to return to work on Monday. This meant sharing her ordeal with her family, given how close they were. *Except Kyla*, Alexa reminded herself, pushing her twin sister's name out of her mind. Thinking of Kyla only deepened her grief.

Focus on wellness. Focus on family—or what's left of it, she told herself.

* * *

The late Saturday afternoon sun cast a warm glow through the windows of the family farmhouse, but Alexa felt cold inside. Perched on the edge of the couch, her hands trembled as she twisted a loose thread on her sleeve. Her mother, Jennie, sat across from her, concern etched on her face.

"I was exhausted, Mom," Alexa whispered, her gaze drifting to the floor before meeting her mother's eyes. "Riding through that storm on Thursday after work took everything out of me.

When I got home, I could only think about finding something to eat. I saw the loaf of bread in the freezer, wrapped just like Grandma's banana bread." Alexa paused, the memory knotting her stomach. "I didn't even think twice. I toasted a thick slice, slathered it with butter, and ate it."

She looked away, her voice trembling. "Soon after, I began to feel strange. At first, it was just a bit of lightheadedness. I thought maybe it was from being tired. But then it got worse."

Alexa stared blankly at the wall as if replaying the scene in her mind. "Feeling a little better after resting, I stepped out onto the balcony. The air was fresh after the rain, and the clear sky was dotted with twinkling stars. It should have felt peaceful, but I still felt off—like I was floating, not quite in my own body. I glanced down the stairwell to the parking level below, and suddenly everything spun. My balance just went, and I tumbled down the stairs, hitting my head against the concrete."

Alexa shivered, her voice catching. "When I came to, I was alone and in pain, completely disoriented."

She observed her mother lean forward, her expression filled with anxiety."Why didn't you call me, dear?" Jennie asked.

"I could barely think straight, Mom. I somehow managed to crawl back to my apartment and get into bed where I stayed most of the next day."

"And now you know the bread affected you that way?" Jennie asked.

Alexa nodded, anger flashing in her eyes. "It wasn't Grandma's bread, Mom. Kyla put it there without telling me. I can't believe she'd do this. My own sister." Alexa took a shaky breath. "I'm so furious—I don't know how I'll face her after this."

The enormity of what Kyla had done hung in the room like a shadow, dark and inescapable. Alexa's mind raced, tangled in a mess of emotions—betrayal, anger, confusion. Kyla had always been her closest confidante, and yet this? *What was she thinking?*

"Sweetheart," Jennie asked, "have you gone for a medical checkup, you know, just to be sure there isn't any damage that isn't apparent to you right now?"

Alexa smiled weakly. "I know, Mom, I knew you'd ask that."

"Well?" Jennie persisted.

Alexa hesitated, her hand moving subconsciously to her temple, where a faint bruise still ached. "I'll make an appointment with Dr. Shelley as soon as I get back home, I promise. But honestly, I think the greatest damage now is that between Kyla and me."

Chapter Five

On Friday at the Goldenrod Retreat, Kyla woke up at 7:00 a.m., her usual waking hour during the week. But this Friday, she had the rare luxury of not having to report to Dr. Nicholl's veterinary clinic. Knowing the November morning would be chilly, she dressed warmly and slipped out quietly, leaving Raine snoring loudly in her bedroom.

A soft haze hung in the air as the sun began to rise. Wispy clouds drifted lazily across the sky, occasionally parting to reveal a glorious red sphere. The sun's rays cast a gentle glow over the landscape, bathing everything in a soft, ethereal light.

The air was crisp and cool, and Kyla was glad she had risen early. The serene, picturesque scene before her filled her with calm and tranquility.

A weathered wooden bench, perfectly placed on the clifftop, offered an ideal spot to watch the day come to life. Kyla inhaled the crisp morning air deeply, feeling rejuvenated after a restful night's sleep. She looked forward to breakfast, where she and Raine would join the other attendees. As Kyla relaxed on the bench, she thought about how much Alexa would enjoy Cortes Island. She was fairly certain Alexa had never visited, let alone stayed overnight.

Alexa! Instantly, a jolt of realization hit Kyla. *Oh, I completely forgot to text her about the package in her freezer.* Kyla recalled that the freezer had been nearly empty, except for an ice-cube tray, and she was pretty sure Alexa wouldn't have any reason to open it unless she'd bought groceries that needed freezing.

What's the worst that can happen? Kyla asked herself. *Alexa might unwrap the foil and, if it looked edible, maybe taste it. Not the end of the world. But it wasn't like her to dig into something she didn't even know was there.*

Still, Kyla didn't want to take any chances. She would make sure to let Alexa know the foil-wrapped item belonged to Raine and was meant for her birthday. Choosing the microphone over typing, Kyla spoke her message, knowing she had too much to say to fit in a text.

"Hey, Alexa! Just wanted to let you know not to open the package in your freezer. It's Raine's—she picked it up from the post office before we caught the ferry yesterday. It's a birthday gift from her brother in Oregon and needs to stay cold. I knew you wouldn't mind, and honestly, even if you opened it or had some—if it's a loaf and you were hungry—it's all good. I meant to text you yesterday, so it's my bad. Not a big deal, and I'm sure Raine would understand. We'll grab it on Sunday evening if that works, or I can get it on Monday if it's too late. No stress. See you soon! Love you!"

* * *

"No worries, Raine. I'll get the package from Alexa's freezer on Monday after work," Kyla said, "or Sunday night if it's not too late."

"Good," Raine replied. "I'll have my gift on my actual birthday, then," she said, twirling with her arms held high in the air. "Maybe I'll even share it with you, Sundance."

Kyla couldn't help but notice a strange glint in Raine's eye, like she was holding back a secret—or a joke only she understood. *Was Raine just excited about her birthday, or was there something more to it?* Kyla brushed off the uneasy feeling, chalking it up to Raine's quirky nature.

The rest of the weekend passed in a blur of meditation sessions and quiet walks along the rugged coastline. By the time Kyla and Raine returned to EarthSong on Sunday evening, it was too late to retrieve Raine's birthday gift from Alexa's apartment. With Monday being a workday, Kyla opted not to disturb Alexa's sleep.

Chapter Six

Back at work on Monday morning, during a break at Dr. Nicholl's veterinary clinic, Kyla sent Alexa a quick text:

> Hi Lexi. Mind if I drop in after work and pick up that package? If I don't see you biking home, I'll head over to your place and see you there, okay?

There was no reply to Kyla's text. Since Kyla had her own key, it wasn't essential for Alexa to be home, although Kyla couldn't wait to catch her up on their trip to Cortes Island, especially its beauty. She knew Alexa would love Cortes.

* * *

With no sign of Alexa on her bike ride after work, Kyla continued on her own to Grace Square. Securing her bicycle in the rack, she skipped up the two flights of stairs at the front entrance and knocked on Alexa's door with a rhythmic beat.

After knocking twice, Kyla concluded that Alexa probably stopped off somewhere on the way home. *Since she didn't reply to my text, she may not have known about my plan to pick up the package. Oh, well. Doesn't matter.*

Rifling through her backpack, Kyla found the key, turned it in the lock, and was startled when she was met with a squinty-eyed Alexa staring her in the face.

"Oh, I didn't know you were home, Lexi. Did you get my text?" Kyla asked, her voice rising with surprise.

Kyla's gaze lingered on Alexa, who did not step aside to let her in.

Something about Alexa's posture made Kyla hesitate, her grip tightening on the door knob. She swung the door open wider, hoping to maneuver into the apartment without bumping into her sister, but a creeping unease clouded her plan. Something was off.

"Alexa, you look upset. Did I do something wrong? Am I interrupting something?" Kyla asked, her gaze flicking over Alexa's shoulder, half-expecting to see someone else inside. "I can come back tomorrow if it's a bad time," she added, trying to figure out the tension. She hadn't seen that look on Alexa's face since they were kids fighting over toys.

Alexa's sharp voice echoed through the hallway. "You might have opened my door and found me dead," she snapped.

Kyla followed Alexa's gaze toward the hallway where she saw a handsome man lingering nearby. He had likely overheard more than either of them wanted, Kyla figured. Noticing Alexa's body stiffen, Kyla could sense her sister's irritation spiking though she didn't realize that Dr. Kevin Hunter—Alexa's secret crush—was the last person she wanted over-hearing this. Without saying a word, Alexa reached for the doorknob and quietly closed the door, shutting out prying ears.

Inside the apartment, Kyla's confusion deepened as she

asked, "What are you talking about, Alexa?" Her voice wavered as she took a small step back, creating some distance from her sister, who now seemed like a live wire ready to snap. Alexa's fists were clenched tightly, her voice rising with each word.

"Whatever was in that tea bread you left in my freezer without asking if it was okay—and without even telling me it was laced with drugs..." Alexa's frustration was palpable; she hadn't taken a breath, her anger boiling over.

Kyla's mouth fell open, her eyes widening in disbelief. She staggered back as if physically struck by the force of Alexa's words. "Laced with drugs? Oh, no!" she gasped, pressing her hand to her mouth in a reflexive gesture. Stunned, she stood frozen, hoping the damage would be minimal, though a sinking feeling and Alexa's grim demeanor suggested otherwise.

Kyla felt Alexa's intense gaze burn into her as she pleaded, "Lexi, please believe me. I had no idea what was in that package. Raine didn't unwrap it because she wanted it to be a surprise on her actual birthday. All she knew was that her brother Mark in Oregon said it needed refrigeration. That's it, Lexi."

Kyla watched as the tension in Alexa's brow softened, the tightness in her jaw loosening. The anger that had blazed in Alexa's eyes began to fade, like mist dissolving in the morning sun. Kyla held her breath, hoping that—just maybe—Alexa was starting to believe her.

"Do you mind if we sit for a bit, Lexi?" Kyla asked meekly.

Alexa turned without a word and walked into the living room, the weight of her silence heavy in the air. Kyla hesitated before following, taking a seat across from her sister. From where she sat, Kyla noticed Alexa's tense shoulders slowly easing. As Alexa leaned forward, her expression softened into quiet curiosity, as if listening was beginning to calm the storm within her.

"Raine and I arrived in Fulford with plenty of time to spare," Kyla continued, choosing her words carefully. "Raine decided to check her mailbox, and when she explained her dilemma, I suggested we come here to put the gift in your freezer. We got back to the ferry dock just in time to board."

Kyla paused, her eyes searching Alexa's face for any sign of understanding. She leaned forward, her voice softening. "Lexi, please let me know what happened. Did you get my text at all?"

Alexa let out a bitter scoff. "Hmph," she retorted sharply. "What a joke, Kyla. I got your text after it was all over. Thanks a bunch for that."

Kyla sank back into her chair, feeling the fragile ground she'd gained slip away beneath her. "I'm so sorry, Lexi. I meant to send it as soon as we left your apartment, but I got distracted on our way to board the ferry and then forgot about it until early the next morning."

Kyla shook her head, a deep sigh escaping her lips. It felt like a sharp knife had pierced her soul. If only she'd texted Alexa immediately, maybe this entire ordeal could have been avoided. Kyla's heart felt heavy with guilt, her shoulders sagging. "It's all my fault, Lexi," she confessed, tears welling in her eyes. She couldn't help but imagine the scene after Alexa returned to her apartment after work on Thursday.

Kyla took a deep breath, summoning the courage to ask for the dreaded details. She braced herself as Alexa began to recount the harrowing events. Kyla felt her breath catch as she listened, her fists tightening until her knuckles turned white. The image of Alexa losing her balance and tumbling down the stairs onto the cold concrete floor seared itself into Kyla's mind. Each word was like a knife twisting deeper—the crawling across the floor, the confusion, the sheer terror.

A wave of helplessness washed over Kyla. "Alexa," she whispered, her voice shaky, "I can't even imagine how terrifying that must have been for you." Confronted with the wreckage of a plan gone horribly wrong, Kyla wished she could disappear.

Her gaze locked on Alexa's face, searching for some sign of forgiveness. "Lexi, can you ever forgive me?" she asked softly. The room felt thick with tension, the silence pressing down on Kyla.

When Alexa didn't respond right away, Kyla reached out, gently taking her sister's hand. "You're safe now," she murmured, more to steady herself than to comfort Alexa.

Kyla knew some wounds might never fully heal, but she was determined to stay by Alexa's side, no matter how long it took to rebuild their fractured trust. She understood she had to confront her guilt and find a way to move forward.

But Alexa pulled her hand away, stood up, and said, "It's been a long day, Kyla. Showing up to work after missing a day without any warning to Dr. Cindy..." Alexa stomped toward the front door, muttering, "I'm going to bed early."

Kyla stood and followed Alexa to the door, clutching her shoulder bag. She thought about hugging her sister, offering some small gesture of comfort, but Alexa's demeanor made it clear this wasn't the time.

With a sad smile, Kyla said goodnight and reached for the doorknob, ready to leave.

"Before you go, Kyla," Alexa said, her voice cold, "I want the key to my apartment back. And tell your hippie friend that her so-called gift is in the trash—clearly marked as poison."

Devastation crashed over Kyla like a tidal wave, leaving her feeling as though she'd been handed a life sentence. Her fingers trembled as she reached into her pocket and retrieved her ring of keys. Slowly, she struggled to slide off the apartment key, her eyes stinging with unshed tears. She opened the door and stepped out into the dim hallway without looking back.

Chapter Seven

Alexa still lived in the same second-floor apartment in Grace Square, conveniently next door to the hunky dentist she'd been eyeing for the past five years. Despite Sunrise Island's gossip mill, she had managed to keep her secret passion for Dr. Kevin Hunter under wraps, even from her twin, with whom she shared everything.

Alexa had taken up running after work, hoping to leave behind the lingering shadows of November's drama. She'd fallen off her regular Pilates schedule at the yoga centre in Ganges, just when she needed it most.

As she rounded the corner of the hallway, her heart sank. Of all people—*him.* Dr. Kevin Hunter stood by his door, fiddling with his keys, looking completely put together.

Fantastic. Just who I want to see when I look like I ran through a carwash, she thought, swiping at her forehead, hoping to clear the damp sheen without making it obvious.

Kevin looked up as he placed his key in the door. "Alexa," his voice broke through her thoughts, warm and surprisingly familiar. She glanced up, startled. He knew her name? Her pulse quickened, though from the run or him, she wasn't sure.

"I was worried about you," he said, his tone light but with a hint of concern.

Alexa felt a wave of unease wash over her. This wasn't how she'd imagined finally speaking to her crush. She'd envisioned something different—dinner maybe, something elegant, something where she didn't look like a drowned rat in running gear. Instead, here she was, hair plastered to her forehead, trying to muster a smile. *But at least he knows I exist*, she thought, a flicker of excitement mingling with embarrassment.

"Dr. Hunter," she greeted him, figuring she might as well admit that she knew his name, too. "Worried about me? Why would you be worried?" she asked, her voice higher pitched than usual.

He leaned back slightly, his expression softening. "The last time I saw you, you were in your doorway. There was a bit of yelling. I didn't want to intrude, but you looked unwell, if I'm honest."

Alexa held her breath. The memory surged forward—Kyla showing up on Monday night to retrieve Raine's birthday gift. She'd been trying to hold it together, but in front of him, it felt like the cracks were on full display.

Alexa shifted uncomfortably, struggling to keep her voice steady. "Yeah, that..." She waved a hand dismissively and attempted a small shrug. "Sorry you had to see that. Just... family stuff. Happens to the best of us, right?" Her attempt at nonchalance fell flat, but it was all she could manage.

Kevin's lips curled into a half-smile, his five o'clock shadow catching the light. "Life happens," he said, his tone easy, though his eyes lingered a little longer on her. "You know, it's funny we don't run into each other more, given how close we live."

Alexa nodded, feeling her mind scramble for something

clever to say, but all she could think about was how she was standing there, a sweaty mess, face-to-face with the man she'd spent years quietly admiring. "Yeah," she finally said, her voice softer now. "I was just thinking the same thing."

There was a pause, something unspoken lingering between them, but Alexa couldn't savour it. Not like this. She forced a smile, feeling a growing sense of awkwardness."I'd love to continue this, but I need to get inside and, uh, cool down," she said, gesturing to her sweat-drenched clothes.

Kevin grinned, his eyes crinkling in the corners. "Of course," he said, stepping back toward his door. "Maybe next time we run into each other, it'll be under better circumstances."

Her heart fluttered at the thought, but she forced herself to play it cool. "Here's hoping," she replied, giving him a quick nod before turning toward her apartment, feeling the weight of his gaze as she walked away.

Inside her apartment, Alexa leaned against the door, her legs feeling shaky, the reality of their encounter sinking in. She sat on the hall bench to pull off her shoes and peel off her socks, letting the cool air hit her feet.

Mrs. Hunter, she mused with a grin, though the smile quickly faded. She couldn't deny her longing to share her excitement with Kyla.

* * *

The rain slapped against Alexa's face as she pedaled harder, the wind pushing against her like an invisible hand trying to force her back. Each drop felt like a tiny, cold pinprick pelting her skin. She gritted her teeth, squinting against the downpour, cursing herself for not hitching a ride today. Dr. Cindy's chiropractic clinic, tucked away on Park Drive, felt miles away, not the usual thirty-odd-minute ride. Every crank of the pedals made her legs burn, and she couldn't remember a time when her clothes had felt this drenched.

By the time she finally reached Grace Square, her arms were aching, her legs leaden. She slid off the bike, water streaming off her jacket in rivulets and puddling at her feet as she locked her bike in place. Alexa tugged at the wet fabric of her raincoat, peeling it off with a frustrated huff. The jacket, soaked through, felt heavy in her hands as she shook it out. Water sprayed across the concrete floor of the bike locker. "Better here than inside," she muttered, pushing the damp fabric into her bag.

Reaching into her pocket, her fingers brushed against the empty space where a tissue should've been. She sighed, wiping her face with her sleeve instead, grimacing as the wet fabric rubbed against her skin. "Why don't I ever have a towel?" she grumbled too tired to think of a real answer.

Alexa made her way up the two flights of stairs, the dampness clinging to her like an extra layer of misery. Her sneakers squished against the carpet, the sound annoyingly loud in the otherwise quiet hallway. She hurried toward Apartment #29, hoping to avoid being seen by the occupant of #30. Hungry, exhausted, and sopping wet in areas not shielded by her rain jacket, Alexa was far from her best.

As she struggled to insert her key into the lock, Alexa was startled when her neighbour arrived at his apartment door moments later. She hoped he'd forgotten about that ugly encounter between her and Kyla on Monday night. But how could he?

Dr. Kevin Hunter looked annoyingly dry, Alexa thought, even in his short black windbreaker. *How had he managed that?* Alexa forced a smile, though her soaked-through clothes and dripping hair made it feel more like a grimace.

"Not the best day for a bike ride," Kevin said with a smile, his voice warm, casual, like he hadn't just caught her looking like she'd been swimming fully clothed.

"Nor for a walk across the square," Alexa replied, trying to match his light tone, though her words came out breathless from exhaustion. She wiped her face again, hoping to remove some of the rain still dripping down her cheeks.

Kevin's eyes glinted with amusement as he leaned casually against his doorframe. "Missing your old job at the gallery?" he teased, a playful nudge in his voice.

Alexa let out a tired laugh. "Not exactly, Kevin. Right now, I'm just longing for dinner, a warm fire, and a cozy bed," she said, her voice trailing off as her stomach growled in agreement.

She was about to turn the key in the lock when she realized what she had said. "Kevin." His name slipped out so easily, as if she'd been saying it all her life. Heat rushed to her face. "Oh, sorry. I didn't mean—Dr. Hunter."

His smile widened, his eyes softening. "That's my name, Alexa," Kevin replied, flashing a set of perfectly aligned teeth.

She'd thought of him as 'Kevin' ever since she saw his name on the brass plate below her own dentist's plaque at the clinic in Grace Square.

Alexa's stomach fluttered. "Okay... Kevin," she said. She couldn't help smiling despite the awkwardness. "I feel like I owe you an apology. Every time we run into each other, I'm a mess."

"You're just fine," he said, the sincerity in his voice catching her off guard. "Really." He moved toward his door, his eyes lingering longer than she expected. "See you soon, I hope," he added with a wink.

Quite the smart-ass, aren't you? Alexa thought, smirking to herself as she stepped into her warm apartment. Alexa stood frozen for a moment, replaying the encounter in her mind. She hung her raincoat in the front hall closet, careful to keep it separate from her other jackets. Trudging to her ensuite bathroom, she plugged the bathtub drain and turned on the chrome faucets full blast.

Alexa peeled off her wet clothes, the fabric clinging stubbornly to her skin, and walked naked into the laundry room, tossing them into the washing machine. She didn't care that her socks were balled up or one leg of her pants was turned inside out. Tonight, it didn't matter.

Returning to the bathroom, she shut off the flow of water and stared in the mirror at her reflection, water still glistening in her hair, her cheeks flushed. Her mind drifted back to Kevin's smile, the way he said her name like it was the most natural thing in the world. She wondered what that wink meant, whether there was something more there—or if she was imagining it.

But as she settled into the warm bath, her thoughts turned in a different direction. She reached for her phone, her first instinct to text Kyla. This would have been the moment she'd share with her twin—the exciting "guess who I talked to" moment. But her hand stilled over the screen.

The joy of daydreaming about the handsome dentist was now tinged with a deep sense of loss, knowing she couldn't share it with the one person who used to know her best. Kyla had always been her confidante, the one who understood her like no one else.

She sank deeper into the water, letting the warmth soothe her body, but the vivid scenes of Monday night refused to wash away. Days later, anger bubbled beneath the surface, simmering with each reminder of how easily Kyla had shattered their trust.

Chapter Eight

After a restless night, Kyla managed a few hours of solid sleep before the blaring cellphone alarm jolted her awake. She still felt exhausted.

She tapped the Stop button, avoiding Snooze, as a wave of nausea surged through her. She threw back the blankets and rushed to the bathroom, vomiting into the toilet.

* * *

Kyla slipped through the door of the veterinary clinic and immersed herself in the day's preparations, silently praying that Dr. Nicholls, with his keen perception, wouldn't notice her tear-streaked face.

Dr. Nicholls leaned against the tall bookshelf, brimming with medical textbooks, and sipped his morning coffee.

"Kyla," he remarked without so much as a *good morning,* "you look like you've been crying."

"No," she replied weakly, "just a lot of onion-peeling last night. We were canning pickles and relishes."

"Hmm," Dr. Nicholls murmured, pushing away from the bookshelf and heading toward Treatment Room #3.

Kyla's mind was stuck on the devastating events of the past few days, her grief clinging to her like a stubborn burr. She struggled to focus on her duties, her thoughts drifting endlessly.

The reception desk beckoned, and Kyla shuffled toward it, her eyes scanning the appointment book. Mrs. Thompson's cat needed vaccinations, and Mr. Carey's dog had an ear infection. Routine tasks, yet Kyla's thoughts remained tangled in images that wouldn't let go.

The door swung open, and Mrs. Thompson stepped in, her bright smile a stark contrast to the gloom weighing heavily on Kyla.

"Is Whiskers ready yet?" Mrs. Thompson asked, her voice filled with anticipation.

Kyla snapped out of her daze, remembering that Whiskers needed a vaccine before being released. She forced a smile and nodded. "I'll just give him his vaccine, and he'll be ready to go."

With a heavy heart, Kyla entered the area where pets awaited a reunion with their owners. The fluorescent lights flickered overhead, casting a harsh glow on the sterile tile floor.

Kyla's hands trembled as she prepared the syringe. She glanced at the label, barely registering that the vaccine was for Whiskers. It wasn't until she withdrew the needle that she noticed Mr. Rodriguez—the sleek Siamese—ears flattened, pupils blown wide in feline disbelief. The look he gave her was pure, unmistakable horror—betrayal wrapped in fur.

He let out a low, guttural yowl—more wounded than angry —and darted to the corner of the exam room, chest heaving, sides fluttering with shallow breaths.

Panic surged as Kyla fumbled for the wall phone and dialed Dr. Nicholls' extension. His stern voice crackled through the receiver.

"Kyla, what's the emergency?"

"Dr. Nicholls," Kyla stammered, her voice barely above a whisper. "I—I gave Mr. Rodriguez the vaccine meant for Whiskers. I'm so sorry. It was my fault—I didn't double-check the label."

Seconds later, Dr. Nicholls swept into the room. He examined Mr. Rodriguez, his frown deepening as he listened to the cat's heart, checked his temperature, and pressed gently on his abdomen. Then he turned to Kyla, who stood anxiously by.

"We'll start him on fluids and administer a mild steroid to minimize any potential reaction," he said crisply. "We'll also run a quick blood panel and keep him overnight for observation. He'll likely be fine, but we're not taking any chances."

After a pause, his gaze sharpened. "Kyla, this is unacceptable. We have protocols for a reason. You're fortunate it wasn't a more serious mistake.

Kyla's cheeks burned with shame. She knew she deserved every word. She'd jeopardized Mr. Rodriguez's health because her grief had clouded her judgment.

When the worst of the emergency had passed, Kyla approached Mr. Rodriguez. He was calm now, the tremble in his limbs fading as the meds took hold. She petted his velvety fur, whispering an apology. The cat gazed at her and purred. She felt a connection—one she often experienced with animals. Maybe he could feel the ache deep within her soul. Maybe animals sensed loss better than humans.

* * *

Kyla couldn't wait for four-thirty. She grabbed her sweater and lunch bag, hoping to avoid the end-of-day chats Dr. Nicholls had started a few months ago. These chats sometimes showed a softer side of Mr. Grumpy Pants, but now she wanted to slip away unnoticed after the day's stresses and her well-deserved reprimand.

Kyla's escape plan failed when Dr. Nicholls asked her to sit in the waiting room and locked the front door.

"Just to avoid interruptions," he said, settling into an armchair near Kyla. He got straight to the point by asking, "What's wrong, Kyla?" The simple question broke Kyla's emotional dam. Tears streamed down her cheeks as she buried her face in her hands, her shoulders shaking with sobs. After a day of holding back her grief, she finally let it all out.

A gentle touch on her shoulder startled her—it was Dr. Nicholls, the last person she expected to show empathy. He quickly withdrew his hand, but the gesture surprised her more than embarrassed her.

How could the man she saw as an icicle in human relations show concern for her well-being, especially after her serious clinical error?

Dabbing her face with tissues from the front desk, Kyla imagined smears of black mascara further marring her appearance. Avoiding his stare, she looked down and said, "Can we talk tomorrow? I'm a mess right now. I promise I'll be better — no more mistakes—I'm sorry."

"Of course, Kyla," Dr. Nicholls replied, his face showing a tenderness she hadn't noticed before. The handsome veterinarian paused, allowing Kyla to take in his perfectly combed hair and neatly trimmed mustache, accentuated by his dark-rimmed glasses.

"Look, Kyla," he said softly, "I know you feel bad about today, and of course it can't happen again. But I want you to know..." He looked directly into her eyes, pausing to emphasize his next words.

"You're the best vet assistant I've ever had. I don't always show it, but it's true... until today." He smiled, lightly brushing her shoulder.

"I know whatever upset you is significant enough to interfere with the attention and care I've come to expect from you—and that I value."

Dr. Nicholls paused, his fingers lightly tapping the arm of his chair, his eyes briefly closing as he took a measured breath, clearly reining in his emotions.

Kyla listened, expecting to be fired. Her eyes softened, a small smile forming at his kind words. *If this is the real Dr. Nicholls, let's have more of that,* she thought. As strange as this chat seemed, it was an unexpected distraction from her troubles.

She was drawn back to the conversation as he continued. "Whatever happened is your business. I do not doubt that you'll be back to yourself tomorrow, and we can resume business as usual."

Dr. Nicholls stood up, smoothing his tie. "See you tomorrow," he said, slipping back into his usual business-like demeanor as he headed to his private office.

Chapter Nine

Kyla barely survived the work week. Waking up on Saturday morning at EarthSong, she stretched from head to toe, thankful she didn't have to get up for work. The week had worn her out more than any time since early October, and she had gratefully fallen into a deep sleep. At least this morning, she didn't need to race to the bathroom, retching. *Maybe that late-night grilled cheese sandwich had helped.*

For four years, the clatter of plates and the mix of murmured conversations and laughter in the big shared kitchen were the sounds of Kyla's home away from home.

She had helped build a straw bale shelter for a couple who had lost their home in a fire in the summer of 2018. The project gave her a new sense of community pride and boosted her confidence in her ability to build a shelter, and when the two people she worked with invited her to join the EarthSong community, she jumped at the chance. Kyla knew her mom, Jennie, had doubts, and that Alexa couldn't understand why she wanted to hang out with the 'hippies,' as everyone called them.

Pulling on a moss-coloured cotton skirt and a cream tee, Kyla slipped into her Birkenstocks and headed to the kitchen. She looked forward to her breakfast of oatmeal, fresh goat milk from the farm, and garden raspberries. What she dreaded was breaking the news to Raine about her birthday gift—and worse, what had happened to Alexa. After a restless night and retching before work on Monday, Kyla hadn't stopped to chat when she last saw Raine that morning, even though it was her birthday. Since Raine had been out of town since then, Kyla had managed to dodge the conversation for almost a week.

"Morning, Kyla," Raine chirped, sliding over on the bench of the long picnic table and beckoning Kyla to sit beside her.

"Morning, Raine," Kyla replied, keeping her tone light as she walked to the stove. "I'll grab some oatmeal and be right over." She slowly stirred the pot of oatmeal with a long-handled spoon, using the motion to steady her nerves.

Group members took turns buying groceries in bulk and cooking meals for the community. One of the things Kyla loved most about this lifestyle was not having to cook for herself every day.

Kyla carried a steaming bowl of oatmeal to the picnic table and sat down. She poured fresh goat milk over the porridge, marvelling at the pure whiteness of the thick liquid. Kyla couldn't understand why her mom still bought hormone-laden cow's milk from the grocery store.

Raine's cheerful offer to add raspberries had Kyla nodding with a slight smile, though the weight of the conversation ahead loomed. Before addressing the missing gift, Kyla reminded herself to approach this moment with care and self-respect, just as her friends often urged.

"You know, I'm just going to savour this meal... it's like a little work of art," Kyla said, taking a moment to admire the rustic simplicity of her breakfast.

"I know what you mean," Raine agreed, her eyes sparkling as she filled Kyla's bowl. "There's something special about the colours, the textures, and the fact that it all comes from right here at home. That's worth celebrating."

Kyla spooned up a bite of the now-cooled porridge, the tart raspberries bursting on her tongue. "Mmm, these raspberries taste like they were just picked."

"While you enjoy your breakfast, I'll get started on the clean-up," Raine said, wiping her hands on a tea towel. "Just let me know when you're ready, and we can talk."

At EarthSong, a chore wheel determined daily tasks, with the first person getting the first choice. No one wanted to pour the urine bucket on the fruit trees for fertilizer, and the second least popular chore was cleaning hair out of the drain in the shared shower. Kyla preferred sweeping the lodge, emptying the compost, bringing in wood for fires, and almost anything that got her outside. Today, she likely had the last choice, having favoured sleeping in over getting her preferred tasks on the chore wheel.

* * *

As Kyla and Raine walked from the kitchen to the lodge's front entrance, they passed shelves and stairs lined with squash harvested before the fall rains and set out to dry to prevent mold. The fruit, shaped like gourds and spaghetti squash, created a striking display of colours—blue, green, and orange-striped. Outside the double doors, wheelbarrows overflowed with squash, waiting for someone to sort them.

"Your birthday gift," Kyla began as they sat on a weathered wood bench in the apple orchard, "was thrown in the trash."

Raine's mouth dropped open, her eyes widening as if in surprise. "What do you mean?" she asked, a furrow creasing her forehead. But to Kyla, the reaction felt off—too practiced, too controlled.

"Your brother's gift of tea bread was laced with something so powerful it could have killed my sister." Kyla looked steadily at Raine, determined for her to understand the weight of her words.

"You mean, your sister opened my present and ate it?" Raine asked, her concern more for the gift than its harm, thought Kyla.

"Raine," Kyla managed, "Alexa didn't get my message in time. She didn't know we'd left it in her freezer. When she checked the freezer for something to eat, she saw it there, looking just like a loaf our grandmother might have left as a treat. She said it looked and tasted like our grandma's banana bread."

Raine placed her hand on her chest, her eyes wide. "And?" she asked.

"Your expression tells me you probably know what was in the bread, Raine. And if that's true, you probably know what happened next."

"Is she okay?" asked Raine.

"What do you think?" was all Kyla could manage before bolting from the bench toward the forest toilet. She leaned over the open seat and vomited, the evergreen trees offering a semblance of privacy. Seeing the seeds and undigested red raspberries in the mess, Kyla knew she couldn't face the same breakfast tomorrow.

Kyla slowly walked back to where she'd left Raine, who stood among the apple trees watching her.

"What's with all this retching and vomiting, Sundance?" Raine asked, a frown forming on her forehead. To Kyla, the concern in her voice felt more like curiosity than genuine worry.

"Good question, Raine. People are starting to ask me the same thing."

"How long have you been dashing off to the toilet in the middle of important conversations?" Raine asked, a smirk playing on her lips. Her tone was teasing, but Kyla could sense a hint of something sharper beneath it.

Kyla coughed. "Not too likely," she countered. "I haven't slept with anyone since..."

Kyla stopped cold. *It couldn't possibly be,* she thought, recalling the night with Jude. *I throw caution to the wind just once, and this happens?*

Raine raised her eyebrows, fixing Kyla with a pointed look that seemed to demand her attention, keeping her from veering off-topic. "Look," Kyla said, masking her worry by changing the subject, "I need to tell you what happened last Thursday night."

* * *

Getting ready for bed that night, Kyla reflected on her meeting with Raine. She thought Raine's wide-eyed incredulity and look of alarm might have convinced someone else that she had no idea what was in the package in the freezer, but Kyla wasn't buying it. *Raine's brother wouldn't send her laced tea bread without a warning. If Raine had eaten it unknowingly, she might have faced the same fate as Alexa... or worse.*

Kyla's doubts about Raine's integrity deepened as she replayed Raine's cryptic comment at the Goldenrod retreat—

"Maybe I'll even share it with you"—now struck Kyla as more ominous, a detail she couldn't shake.

Kyla knew she had to stay cordial with Raine—they were part of the same close-knit village and had been friends for a long time. But just how trustworthy Raine truly was remained uncertain. Kyla already had more than enough on her plate.

Chapter Ten

S ince it seemed to help, Kyla decided to make it a habit to eat something before bed… at least until this crazy upset stomach settled down. On Sunday morning, she woke up feeling well but couldn't stand the thought of raspberries. To avoid the kitchen and the inevitable scent, she decided to take a stroll in the fresh air. By suppertime, when she'd help prepare their pasta dinner, all the breakfast food would have been put away.

Outside, Kyla peeked through the wire fence to the chicken yard where a large rooster strutted about like a king. She continued walking past the goats grazing in the pasture and decided she'd call her doctor's office first thing Monday morning. *On second thought*, she decided, *I could pick up a pregnancy test kit at the pharmacy this morning.*

* * *

Kyla's hands trembled as she picked up the pregnancy test kit, her heart pounding with anxiety and her stomach knotted with anticipation.

She took a deep breath, trying to steady herself, and walked into the shared bathroom. The cold from the white tile floor seeped into her bare feet, amplifying the chill spreading through her body. She opened the box and carefully read the instructions, her eyes darting back and forth, trying to absorb every detail. Her fingers fumbled slightly as she took out the test strip. Kyla closed her eyes for a moment, gathering her courage, and then proceeded.

After following the steps, she sat on the wooden chair, test in hand, her breath shallow as she waited. She watched the seconds crawl by on her phone, each one stretching into what felt like an eternity. A knock on the door jolted Kyla back to the present.

"Are you just about done in there?" a female voice inquired through the door.

"Oh, sorry! I'll just need another minute. If you don't mind, could you use the forest toilet?"

"No worries," came the muffled reply, followed by footsteps away from the bathroom.

When the time was finally up, Kyla glanced at the test strip.

Two lines.

Positive.

A wave of emotions crashed over Kyla—shock, fear, disbelief, and a flicker of excitement, all tangled together. Her initial instinct was to double-check the instructions, making sure she hadn't misread them.

But there was no mistake. The test indicated she was pregnant. She would seek confirmation from Dr. Shelley as soon as she could get an appointment.

Kyla's mind raced back to that enchanting moonlit night shared with Jude. Now, the reality of that night stared back at her through two pink lines.

Kyla felt a lump form in her throat as tears welled up in the corners of her eyes. Her hands instinctively went to her abdomen, as if trying to connect with the new life forming inside her.

The thought of having a baby felt overwhelming. Until now, she hadn't regretted that moment of reckless abandon, but suddenly, doubt and uncertainty consumed her.

Not wanting to encounter another person hoping to use the bathroom, Kyla removed a hand towel from the rack. She could use it to hide her face if she met anyone between the bathroom and the bedroom. Otherwise, it would be too hard to hide her emotions and avoid questions.

In her room, Kyla stood with her back to the wall and slowly sank to the floor. She hugged her knees to her chest, her mind a whirlwind of thoughts. *What will I do? Should I try to find Jude?*

Soon, she thought about the path of her own life. *What about my plans? My dreams?*

There were no answers. Everything seemed to blur together and Kyla felt lost, immersed in a sea of conflicting emotions and uncertainty.

Kyla allowed herself to feel everything, just like the village members did when they shared their troubles. They all knew they were there for each other—at least, Kyla reminded herself, *most* conducted themselves that way. But Kyla knew the scale of this problem needed more than support from her ecovillage family.

Amidst the chaos in her mind, Kyla held onto the tiny flicker of hope that her tight-knit family at Cliffhouse would help her through this, just as they always had. She couldn't imagine facing what lay ahead without the support of her family, especially her twin sister.

Chapter Eleven

Although Kyla had convinced herself not to call Alexa today—it was still too soon, too raw after everything that had happened—she couldn't resist. Her heartache refused to be silenced, no matter how much she tried to be practical.

Hearing Alexa's voice on the recorded message, Kyla felt a pang of heartbreak. But she held steady.

"Alexa, can you meet me at the Treehouse in about an hour, please? We need to sort out this horrible misunderstanding. I'm just as devastated as you are..." The beep cut her off. She stared at the phone, her heart pounding. *Maybe it's for the best*, she thought, wiping a tear from her cheek.

Kyla slipped her cellphone into her pocket and headed to the kitchen. The sharp, earthy scent of garlic from the community garden permeated the air, a welcome change from the dreaded urine bucket. She began peeling the cloves, the papery skins crackling under her fingers. After a few minutes, her fingertips turned raw, the skin beneath her thumbnail throbbing. She winced each time garlic juice seeped into the tiny cuts, the sting shooting through her hand.

Depositing the peeled garlic on the kitchen island, Kyla swiped her finger across a streak of honey glistening on the cutting board. Fresh honey was gathered from bees on the property, and she hoped it would help soothe her upset stomach.

Remembering it was her turn to help make dinner tomorrow, Kyla opened the freezer, her breath visible in the cold air, and pulled out a container of homemade pesto. She placed it in the fridge to thaw, the green sauce a reminder of summer's basil harvest. The scent of basil filled her mind, recalling sunlit days spent harvesting the herb. The pesto would transform their winter linguini into a summer feast, though it always led to groans of "I ate too much."

Kyla's fingers fumbled for her phone, its screen glaringly empty. No missed calls, no texts. The ringer was on, yet the phone stayed silent. Her chest tightened, frustration and despair gnawing at her insides. Every minute without a word from Alexa felt like another brick in the wall between them. The silence pressed down on her, an ache of loss and unspoken words. Kyla's heart clenched, realizing something precious had slipped away, maybe forever. She longed for the days when they could talk about anything.

Kyla stepped outside, the cool air a relief on her heated skin, and headed toward the fruit orchard. A door slammed shut in the upper tier of the nearby family unit, drawing her attention.

"Hey, Sundance," Lily's voice called from above. Lily, a WWOOF member, worked on organic farms like EarthSong in exchange for food and lodging, just as Jude did.

Kyla glanced up at Lily, marvelling at how their community had blossomed into a vibrant tapestry of people from around the globe. When asked to help manage the community, Kyla had hesitated, the weight of responsibility heavy alongside her full-time job at the vet clinic.

Kyla waved at Lily, her mood too heavy for company. She reached for a ripe ambrosia apple, but the churning in her stomach made her drop her arm to her side. Her mouth watered at the thought of biting into its sharp acidity.

Walking deep into the fruit orchard, Kyla sank into a hand-made chair crafted from bent willow branches at the farm. She pulled her wool sweater tighter and buttoned it against the chill in the shade; even with the patchy sunlight, it was already mid-November, and the air was brisk.

Lily stepped out of her house, her presence stirring a memory of Jude. Kyla's thoughts drifted to that evening in early October, standing on the seashore with Jude under the moonlight. With his shirt off, Jude's physique had taken Kyla's breath away, and she couldn't resist him, no matter how hard she tried. His long, unruly blond hair caught the silver light, and his striking blue eyes held a captivating intensity.

As she sat on the bentwood chair, Kyla shook her head, reflecting on her behaviour that night. One-night stands were completely out of character for her—something she'd never done until that night.

At twenty-four, having spent her entire life on Sunrise Island, Kyla sometimes wondered what she might be missing. Her relationship history included a handful of longer-term relationships since she was sixteen, but nothing to consider marriage

At EarthSong, drinking wasn't a big thing. People had the occasional beer or cider made from the apples in the orchard. Kyla smiled to herself, thinking she might have had one beer too many that night. Since she rarely drank, it didn't take much for her to get tipsy. Jude had offered her a puff from his cannabis cigarette, but Kyla didn't smoke. Maybe she'd decided to throw caution to the wind. After all, life was short—something she was all too aware of since her father Derrick had passed away at just forty-four years of age.

Jude was gone the next morning. Kyla knew he was leaving, and maybe that made everything between them feel more intense, more urgent. *It felt like passion, anyway.* In the wake of it all, Kyla didn't have any regrets. If she listened to her heart, there was a nagging sense of longing. She couldn't shake the thought that if Jude ever came back to EarthSong, she'd want to pick up where they left off—wherever that was.

But now, there was something else weighing on Kyla. A new concern had emerged, adding a whole new layer to the story of that night in early October.

Chapter Twelve

Jennie drew in a deep breath of crisp November air, her steps light as a burst of cheerfulness bubbled up inside her. "Mom, isn't this a gorgeous day?" she called out, trying to lift her mother's spirits.

Kathleen nodded, her lips curving into a faint smile. "It is, dear. I was wondering if the girls might come over for a visit next weekend. What do you think?" Her voice wavered slightly as they walked side by side, Kathleen's steps slower than Jennie would've liked to see. Jennie couldn't help but notice the uneven rhythm of her mother's gait as they made their way down the woodchip trail toward the henhouse, the egg basket swaying in Kathleen's grip.

A tightness crept into Jennie's chest, each faltering step tugging at her heart. It wasn't just age that was slowing her mother down; it was the toll of everything that had happened recently. Alexa's ordeal with the laced tea bread had shaken them all, but it seemed to have hit Kathleen the hardest. Jennie had seen her kneading dough, her mother's hands moving mechanically through the motions, but the life that once fueled every movement seemed to have drained away. Jennie could see her mother pushing herself, every step deliberate and careful, the weight of recent events visible in the way her shoulders slumped and her eyes dulled with fatigue.

Jennie reached out, giving Kathleen's arm a reassuring squeeze. "I know you're worried about all of it, Mom. Clay and I talked last night, and we think it's best if they work this out on their own." She tried to sound confident, even though she wasn't entirely sure herself. "Some things, we just can't fix, no matter how much we want to."

Kathleen's eyes narrowed slightly, her jaw set in that familiar way that told Jennie her mother wasn't backing down. "I disagree, Jen," Kathleen said, lifting her chin defiantly. "There are few things a slow-roasted beef and a homemade cherry pie can't resolve."

Jennie chuckled softly, caught between admiration and concern. Kathleen had always believed in the power of gathering the family around a good meal, but this one felt different. "Alright, Mom, I'll give Alexa a call," she conceded. "But it has to be Alexa. Of the two, she's the one who might turn down our invitation because of what happened. She's still carrying a lot, and she might not be ready yet.

She saw a flicker of concern in Kathleen's eyes, mirroring her own. As much as Jennie wanted to believe a family dinner could make things right, she couldn't ignore the seriousness of what they were dealing with.

* * *

Jennie's pulse quickened with both hope and dread. She'd been anxious about this call, hoping to bridge the growing gap between her daughters. She pressed the call button and waited, bracing herself for whatever might come.

"Hi, Mom." Alexa's voice came through strong and clear, a small relief to Jennie's frayed nerves.

Jennie drew in a slow breath, forcing a lightness into her voice that didn't quite match the tightness in her chest. "Alexa, sweetheart, what's going on with you this Sunday afternoon?"

"Oh, just sitting here on the dock swinging my legs like a little kid," Alexa replied with a wry laugh. "And frankly, I'm just glad to be alive after what happened last Thursday night."

A sharp ache stabbed at Jennie's heart as Alexa's words hit her with blunt force, the reality of the ordeal surfacing immediately. "Yes, I know, Lexi," Jennie said, her voice softening. "It's going to take some time to process all of that. It was more than just physically harmful—it was mentally and emotionally exhausting, too. It's not something you'll just get over in a few days."

"A few days, Mom?" Alexa's voice sharpened, slicing through the conversation with a frustrated edge that hung heavy in the air. "I may never get over this. I'll never forget it."

Jennie nodded, even though Alexa couldn't see her. She could feel the emotion rising on the other end of the line and worked to keep her voice steady. "I wasn't suggesting you'd forget, darling. How could you?"

"I wish it had never happened," Alexa said, her voice tight. "But it did. And now I'm dealing with the consequences."

Jennie paused, her mind racing as she weighed her next words, careful not to press too hard against the raw edges of Alexa's emotions. "How are you feeling physically, dear? Any more headaches? Are your injuries healing well?"

"Healing well enough," Alexa said. "That gash on the side of my head is taking its time, but the scrapes and bruises on my arms and legs are doing okay. My right wrist has been sore, though. I guess I tried to break my fall, but it wasn't enough."

Jennie let out a slow, measured breath, feeling a small sense of relief at the hopeful tone in Alexa's words. "I'm glad to hear you're making progress, Lex," she said, trying to keep her tone upbeat. "Listen, dear," she began carefully, "Mom wants to invite you and Kyla for dinner next Sunday. She's making pot roast and one of her famous cherry pies."

The silence that followed was thick, each passing second stretching into what felt like minutes, the weight of unspoken thoughts filling the space between them.

"Please tell Grandma I appreciate the invite and that I'll visit Cliffhouse soon," Alexa finally said, her voice picking up a little. "Tell Grandma I miss her and hope she can overnight in my apartment before Christmas."

Jennie's heart softened. "I will, dear. Mom gets anxious if she hasn't seen you and Kyla for a while, you know."

"Aw," Alexa murmured. "I know, she's eighty-four now, right? Every day is precious."

The tight knot of tension in Jennie's shoulders eased slightly as Alexa's tone softened, though the underlying worry still lingered just beneath the surface. The conversation had lightened, but there was still one thing she needed to say. "Lex," she ventured, her voice gentle, "don't you think it's time for you and Kyla to talk about what happened? You two were so close."

"I know, Mom, but you don't understand," Alexa said, her tone hardening. "None of this would have happened if Kyla hadn't invited a stranger into my apartment without my permission. That alone is enough to upset me, but this..."

Jennie nodded, her fingers gripping the phone a little tighter as she swallowed the surge of frustration that threatened to spill out. "Yes, I can see why you'd be upset by that, dear. I would be too."

"I gave her a key because I trusted her, Mom. It was for her convenience, not to let strangers into my home."

"I get it, Lex, I do," Jennie said softly, choosing her next words carefully. "You know Kyla had no idea about the tea bread. She didn't even realize it was food, let alone that you'd eat it."

"I don't know what was going through her thick head," Alexa snapped, her voice sharp. "Any fool would know not to leave something in somebody's freezer without knowing what it was—or mentioning it—especially when it's something like that."

Jennie parted her lips to speak, but Alexa's words tumbled out, fast and raw, leaving no space for interruption. "Kyla sent me a text after the fact, I didn't even see it until the next morning."

"What terrible timing," Jennie murmured, still reeling from the weight of Alexa's story and the toll it had taken on her.

"It's not about bad luck, Mom. It's about responsibility," Alexa snapped, her voice tight with anger, each word sharp and deliberate.

Jennie inhaled deeply, her mind scrambling to find the delicate balance between understanding and pushing too far. "I'm not defending what Kyla did, Lex, but she did try to inform you. She had no idea the gift was dangerous, and she couldn't have known you'd open and taste it right away."

"Mom, I have to go," Alexa said abruptly. "Thanks for calling and for the invite." Her voice softened slightly. "You're right about one thing—this is between Kyla and me. That's all I have to say."

"Okay, dear. I understand. Thanks for the chat. Love you."

"I love you too, Mom," Alexa replied, her voice gentler. "And please give Grandma a big hug from me."

As Jennie ended the call, a heavy weight settled over her chest, the unresolved tension between her daughters pressing down harder than ever. She knew this wasn't over, not by a long shot. But she also knew she'd keep trying—for Alexa, Kyla, and the family she was determined to hold together.

Chapter Thirteen

Bev's bright red hair flared like a beacon, drawing Jennie's attention the moment she stepped into the dimly lit Treehouse café. *Typical Bev*, Jennie thought, a smile spreading across her face.

"Jennie! I got here early and snagged the biggest table so we can spread everything out," Bev announced, her voice lively as ever, skipping over the usual pleasantries.

Jennie let out a soft laugh as she approached, her heart warming at the sight of Bev already bustling with energy. Bev rose to meet her with an enthusiastic hug, and Jennie welcomed the familiar comfort.

"That's wonderful," Jennie replied, holding Bev close while securing her wide-brimmed hat against the impact of the hug. "I've got some new ideas I want to run past you."

Jennie settled onto the solid wood bench and plopped her handbag beside her. Eyeing the heart design drawn in the foam on Bev's coffee, Jennie smiled. "You know, Bev, it seems like everything's coming together in my life."

"Ah, Jen, it makes me so happy to hear you say that but, you know, I can see it," Bev smiled with delight.

"There's Clay, of course. You lived that whole story alongside me, dear friend, and I couldn't feel more blessed." Jennie's throat tightened, her eyes misting as she felt the depth of Bev's loyalty.

After placing her order for a soy latte, Jennie smiled and said, "Nick graduates from CMCC next spring, and he seems to be in a stable relationship."

"That's just marvellous, Jen. And what about Lexi and Kyla?" Bev inquired. "I haven't seen them for far too long."

Jennie's children called her "Aunt Bev" though she wasn't a blood relative. Long divorced and without children of her own, Bev had showered affection on Jennie and Derrick's kids, watching them grow up since the family first moved to Sunrise in 2001.

Jennie paused, her fingers tracing the rim of her cup before answering. "Oh, they're fine, Bev, thank you. Alexa loves her job at the chiro clinic, and Kyla enjoys hers though she's not a fan of Dr. Nicholls. He's not all bad, she says, and he's the most popular vet in town because he's the only vet in town."

They both chuckled at Kyla's joke, but Bev wanted to dig deeper. Jennie knew full well that her dearest friend didn't miss a thing.

"So," Bev said with a wink, "what are you not telling me?"

"Ha, Bev," responded Jen. "I can't slip anything by you, can I?"

"Nope."

The arrival of Jennie's steaming latte gave her a brief respite, a moment to gather her thoughts. She admired the triple tulip design in her cup. "There you go, Bev, three tulips for my three adult children. What could be more appropriate?"

"Perfect," replied Bev. "Now, what's up?"

"Oh, nothing that a little time and TLC won't fix, I imagine," Jennie began. "It's just that Lex and Kyla had a falling out a couple of weeks ago, and I don't think it's something that's going to be mended anytime soon."

"Oh, that's surprising, Jen. The twins have always been so close. I don't think I ever remember them scrapping—except maybe when they were kids fighting over who gets the biggest piece of cake, or something."

"That's true, Bev, but I have to say that this was a really unfortunate mishap."

Jennie recounted the story, watching as Bev's lively expression faded, replaced by quiet shock. When she finished, Jennie gave her friend a wistful look and shrugged. "They have to work it out themselves."

"That's shocking. I'm so sorry to hear this. Most of all, I'm so glad that Lexi is alright."

"I know. There could have been a different ending. When you think of it that way, their present issue seems tame. But I have to admit that the rift has had a ripple effect on the family. I mean, we didn't mention it to Nick. No need to upset him. And hopefully, it'll all be resolved well before Christmas."

"Yes. That's less than five weeks from now. Surely things will be back to normal by then." Bev paused, eyes downcast, betraying her uncertainty.

Jen looked into her bag and pulled out a journal of her ideas for the Christmas market. Happy to leave the topic of sisterly discord behind, Jennie had no idea that the current situation paled compared to what she was about to learn.

Chapter Fourteen

With just two-and-a-half weeks until the Christmas market's opening, Jennie and Bev worked in perfect sync, ensuring everything would be ready for Saturday, December 17. After twenty years of running the market together, this year felt different—Covid restrictions had been lifted only two months ago.

The indoor market was just as iconic as the popular open-air summer market but less well-known to outsiders. Before the pandemic, crafters would transition their wares indoors as soon as the open-air market closed in October. But Covid had changed everything, including shutting down the market entirely for two years.

With more time spent at home, crafters produced more than ever. The sheer volume of handmade goods threatened to overwhelm the market building, so Jennie and Bev added an outdoor area for the first time.

As they watched the crafters arrive with their creations, they saw the impact of the past few years—some pieces reflected hardship, while others radiated hope.

* * *

Jennie bounded up the five wood steps to the crafts building and swung open the front door. Scanning the room, she spotted Bev studying a paper on her clipboard as she moved among the stalls rented by crafters. Jennie and Bev expected some crafters would rush in at the last minute and set up on Saturday morning just before the 10:00 a.m. opening. There would be the usual jokes about their 'running on island time,' but Bev and Jennie wanted to preserve the community culture without imposing too many rules.

But they were not ones to leave things to chance, even if others did. Everything had to be meticulously prepared in advance to guard against potential issues. A little rusty after the two-year break, Jennie and Bev were more vigilant than ever.

"Hey, Bev, lookin' good so far." Jennie greeted her friend with a burst of enthusiasm. Over 200 crafters, from Sunrise Island to Alberta, were on the list this year. With customers eager to resume pre-pandemic lives, a big turnout was expected and they needed to be ready.

"Yes, so far, so good," Bev replied with a smile. "But there's one thing I'm concerned about, Jen," she added, her smile fading into a frown.

Jennie listened intently, ready to tackle any perceived problems as they arose. "What is it, Bev?" she asked confidently.

"Our paper supplies haven't arrived yet. I ordered them on November 1st."

"Yikes, a month late. Not surprising given the supply chain issues over the last two years." Jennie pondered for a moment. "I'll give them a call, see if I can somehow expedite delivery," she said. Heading toward their tiny office, Jennie considered the consequences if the paper supplies didn't arrive in time.

After a short while, Jennie rejoined Bev with an update. "I couldn't get through," she said, her lips downturned.

"Ah," replied Bev. "Why am I not surprised?"

"I know," agreed Jennie. "We're not the only pebble on the beach, as my father used to say."

They shared a brief chuckle until reality set in. "Can you imagine having no toilet paper with hordes of people swarming the building?" asked Jennie.

"Horror story," replied Bev. "I can just see a parade of visitors heading toward Grace Square, hoping there's a bathroom in the grocery store."

"I know of some who might just use a broad leaf found in the forest," Jennie said, adding some humor to the situation. Glancing around the hall, Jennie sensed that this might be her moment to suggest they ask Kyla and Alexa to help.

"Hey, Bev; I've been thinking," Jennie began. "I know we pride ourselves on being the sole organizers of the indoor market, but his year is different."

Before she could continue, Bev cut in. "Yes, Jen; I think we could use some help. What did you have in mind?"

"I'd like to ask the twins if they could spare some time to help out" Jennie replied, pleased she didn't have to convince Bev that help was needed.

Bev's eyes lit up. "Ah, my two favourite girls. Let's get them in on this. Maybe they could help organize the outdoor area."

They compiled a list of jobs the girls might help with. "Hmm," Jennie said, already scheming how to get the girls in the same space, "putting up Christmas lights usually takes two people..."

* * *

Jennie stood in the crisp morning air, the scent of pine and cinnamon drifting from the half-set-up stalls at the Christmas market. Twinkling fairy lights hung limply, waiting for someone to string them properly, and the large red and white canopy for Santa's booth flapped weakly in the breeze. Jennie surveyed the scene, her white Audi parked nearby, and glanced at her watch. The twins were late.

When Kyla and Alexa finally arrived, Jennie could feel the tension between them like an icy gust. Kyla's face was tight, her gaze fixed anywhere but on her sister, while Alexa frowned sharply, arms locked across her chest. Jennie felt a pang of frustration but pushed it aside. This was her chance. Maybe, just maybe, this shared task would bring them back together.

"Good morning, girls," Jennie said, her attempt at cheerfulness sounding hollow even to herself.

"I could use some extra hands today. I thought we could all pitch in and make the market really special."

Kyla nodded mutely, her gaze fixed somewhere past Jennie's shoulder, while Alexa merely shrugged, her expression unmoved.

"Right, well, Kyla, I need you to help set up the display for the gingerbread contest. The stands are over there, and we've got some wreaths to hang around them—make it look festive."

Kyla gave a curt nod, barely meeting Jennie's eyes, and headed off without a word, her footsteps crunching on the frosty grass.

Jennie took a steadying breath.

"And Alexa," she said, shifting her focus to her other daughter, "could you hang these lights around the stalls? It'll look magical once it gets dark."

Alexa took the bundle of lights, her fingers gripping it too tightly. She flicked a glance toward Kyla, then back to Jennie. "Sure. Whatever."

Jennie watched them split off in opposite directions, her heart sinking. She tried to busy herself with unpacking the holiday banners, but her eyes kept drifting back. Kyla struggled with a large wreath, balancing it awkwardly on the stand, while Alexa, clearly frustrated, muttered to herself, fighting with the tangled lights.

After a few minutes, Jennie walked over to Alexa, ready to lend a hand. "Need some help with that?"

"I'm fine," Alexa snapped, not looking up. She yanked the string of lights, and a bulb shattered on the ground, the sharp sound cutting through the festive music playing from the speakers. Alexa cursed under her breath and kicked the broken bulb aside, her frustration spilling over.

Jennie sighed and turned to check on Kyla, who was now balancing on a stool, trying to hang a garland. Jennie's pulse quickened when she saw the stool wobble, and she rushed forward. "Be careful, Kyla! You don't need to do it all by yourself."

Kyla steadied herself, her jaw tight. "I've got it, Mom. I don't need any help."

After a few minutes, Jennie walked over to Alexa. 'Need some help with that?'

When Alexa snapped at her, Jennie stepped back, her attempts at peacemaking slipping through her fingers.

She could see the hurt simmering in Alexa's eyes, the cold determination in Kyla's movements. The market was coming together, but it felt like her family was falling apart.

She glanced at Alexa, who was now glaring at the lights like they were the enemy. "Alexa, why don't you help Kyla with the wreaths? It'll go faster if you ..."

"No," Alexa interrupted, her voice sharp. "I'll do the lights. Alone." She emphasized the last word, shooting a glance at Kyla, who didn't even flinch.

Jennie pressed her lips together, a knot forming in her stomach. This wasn't the reunion she had imagined—no laughter, no shared moments. Just icy silence and the sound of decorations clattering into place.

Bev's voice pulled her from her thoughts. "This is like watching a train wreck in slow motion," Bev said, shaking her head.

Jennie exhaled slowly, her chest tightening. "I thought being here, working together, would remind them of all the good times we've had together setting up for community events over the years."

Jennie felt the comfort of Bev's hand on her shoulder. "They're hurting, Jen. And sometimes, it takes more than shared memories and a little Christmas spirit to fix that."

Jennie felt Bev's squeeze on her shoulder, listening to her wise words, "They just need time."

Jennie nodded, though her heart felt like it was splintering. "I just hope they'll realize how much they need each other before it's too late."

As the morning dragged on, Jennie watched her daughters work, two islands drifting farther apart, each refusing to bridge the gap. Her heart ached as she realized that mending their bond wouldn't be as simple as hanging a string of lights or arranging a festive display. She realized it would take more than a festive market to bring them back together.

Jennie sighed, pulling her coat tighter around her. The market would be beautiful when it was finished, but today, all she could see were the frayed edges of her family, struggling to hold together against the bitter cold.

Chapter Fifteen

Cliffhouse by the Sea, Jennie's once thriving B&B, now sat quieter than she ever thought possible. The pandemic had drained the usual steady flow of visitors, leaving the place to feel more like a private retreat. But life had shifted in deeper ways too—Clay's accident had made him a fixture here. Jennie could still picture the early days after the crash, her heart heavy with worry as she cared for him. Now, three years later, she couldn't imagine the house without him.

She glanced across the verandah, where their coffee cups steamed in the cool air, and her eyes softened at the sight of Clay sipping his drink. The sky hung heavy and gray like it had for days, but the air still held a crispness she found invigorating. She thought back to when Clay first moved in, his presence filling the empty spaces that the pandemic had left behind. Now, his things were as much a part of Cliffhouse as the worn chairs they were sitting in.

Can you believe it's been over four-and-a-half years since I closed the B&B, Clay?" Jennie mused, her gaze drifting toward the distant sea.

"I can," Clay replied, rising from his chair to join her by the railing. "Have you thought about starting it up again? Or have you considered renting the units out yearly, like I suggested?"

Jennie nodded, her mind wandering to all the possibilities. "Year-round rentals would be far easier than running the B&B. Besides, I've been thinking Kyla might want one of them." The idea hung between them, filled with the unspoken hope that Kyla would come home for good.

Clay raised an eyebrow, a slow smile playing on his lips. "Bring her back into the fold?"

"That's the plan." Jennie's voice was determined. "Maybe, if she's here, it won't be so easy for her and Alexa to avoid each other."

Clay chuckled, his eyes glinting with amusement. "Smart move, Mama."

Jennie smiled, yet a hint of uncertainty clouded her face. "I know I can't force it but that doesn't mean I can't help it along. I just want them to remember how much they mean to each other."

"And you'd be happy to see Kyla away from that commune?" Clay asked, watching her closely.

Jennie sighed, her shoulders drooping with the weight of her thoughts. "It's not the commune that worries me. It's the distance between the girls that does."

Clay's arm slipped around her, and Jennie leaned into the warmth of his familiar embrace. His voice rumbled beside her. "If Kyla moves back, she'll need a car for that long commute."

Jennie's eyes twinkled with a sudden idea. "That's where you come in," she teased, her smile brightening.

Clay laughed. "I'll help her find something reliable. And I'll make sure she knows how to take care of it."

Jennie's heart lightened at the thought, her mind already ticking through all the ways she could nudge her girls back together. "It would give her some independence. But I wish there was a way to help her leave that vet clinic. I know she loves the work, but her boss..."

Clay shrugged, a trace of amusement in his expression. "Not everyone gets to be their own grumpy boss like me."

Jennie chuckled, though her thoughts stayed on Kyla. "Maybe there's something she could do here on the farm. It could be what she needs to make a change."

Clay surveyed the grounds. Though it was winter, and everything looked dormant, Jennie knew there was always work to be done. "I can think of a million things she could do around here. The fences need mending, for starters. If she isn't handy, she could learn... "

Clay's eyes followed hers as they scanned the property. Even in the quiet of winter, there was always something that needed tending. "Plenty of work to go around here, that's for sure. The fences are a start."

Jennie's eyes softened with a memory. "She was so proud when she helped build that straw bale shelter with people from EarthSong. And her dad taught her to chop wood—she'd be a real asset here."

"She'd fit right in," Clay agreed, his tone warm.

Jennie felt a glimmer of hope rise within her. "Maybe I'll talk to her. See what she thinks."

Clay squeezed her shoulder gently, his steady presence grounding her. "Just don't get so wrapped up in fixing things that you forget to enjoy what's in front of you."

Jennie smiled, leaning into the comfort of his words. "Speaking of enjoying things, I'm meeting Bev at the Treehouse Café this afternoon. We've got a few last-minute Christmas Market details to go over."

Clay raised an eyebrow at the thick clouds rolling in.

"You've got a deadline looming, don't you? The market's soon, right?"

Jennie chuckled softly. "December 17. Just around the corner."

Clay's knowing look made her heart warm. "Maybe you could get your twin daughters to lend a hand."

Jennie's smile faltered briefly as memories of their last attempt washed over her. "We tried that already, but it didn't go well." She shook her head, trying to let go of the weight of that day. "But don't worry, dear, Bev and I have been planning this for months. Today's just about finalizing things."

Clay grinned, his admiration for her always shining through.

Jennie returned the smile, feeling the warmth of his compliment as he leaned in to give her a quick kiss. She watched as he turned and headed down the verandah steps, calling for Rollo. The sight of Clay with Rollo never failed to bring a sense of peace. Their beloved German pointer had been a steadfast part of their family since he was a puppy.

Jennie watched as Rollo bounded toward Clay. "Hey, big fella," Clay called, greeting their beloved German pointer with a vigorous rub. At fourteen, Rollo was still spry enough to keep up with Clay's every move. Jennie smiled, recalling how Rollo had been a steady presence during the twins' most difficult years. Though he came to them as a newborn rescue, it often felt like Rollo had been the one doing the rescuing, offering the twins and Nick quiet comfort in their hardest moments, with an understanding that never needed words. "If all else fails," Jennie called out with a half-smile, "maybe Rollo can work his magic and bring Kyla and Alexa back together."

Clay laughed, waving as he disappeared down the steps, Rollo at his side. Jennie watched them head toward the fields, feeling her spirits lift. Rollo had always been there when they needed him most—maybe he still had one more miracle left in him.

Chapter Sixteen

Alexa barely made it through the workweek, burying herself in tasks that kept her away from Kyla. She lingered at the office after hours, tidying the front desk and replacing the face paper on the chiropractic tables—mundane chores that gave her the buffer she needed. A twenty-minute delay was enough to dodge Kyla on the bike ride home, avoiding that awkward, inevitable encounter.

With her backpack secured, Alexa mounted her bike and pedaled away from the clinic, the cool evening air brushing against her tired face. She merged onto the main road, feeling her muscles engage with each turn of the pedals. As she approached the familiar side street where she and Kyla used to catch up, she found her eyes drifting down the road toward the veterinary clinic. Something made her slow—a figure slumped near a fallen bike. Holding her breath, Alexa squinted, trying to sharpen her focus. *Is that Kyla?*

The thought jolted through Alexa's mind, quick and sharp. She veered to the side of the road, her feet hitting the gravel. She peered down the road, trying to make sense of what she was looking at. The hair, the clothes—it had to be her. Panic surged as she pedaled hard toward the figure, hoping, praying she was wrong. *Please don't let it be her; please let her be okay.* When she reached Kyla, Alexa's breath caught. Her sister lay still, crumpled on the ground, looking so vulnerable, so unlike herself.

"Kyla!" Alexa's voice trembled as she crouched beside her, scanning her sister's face for any sign of injury. Her relief was swift when Kyla's eyes fluttered open.

"Oh, thank God," Alexa exhaled, her hands shaking. "Where does it hurt? Can you move?"

Kyla didn't respond. She lay sprawled on the gravel, eyes glassy, tears threatening to spill. Alexa's heartbeat thrummed in her ears as she slipped off her coat and set it beside her.

"It's okay," she murmured, kneeling close. "Take your time."

Kyla drew a long, shaky breath. Slowly, she tucked her chin and bent her left knee, grimacing as she managed to sit up. Alexa gently wrapped the coat around her shoulders, then stood to move the fallen bike to the side of the road.

She sat beside Kyla, who had buried her face in her hands, sobbing quietly. Alexa's eyes scanned Kyla's body, checking again for any sign of injury she might have missed. She stayed close but didn't press; she knew Kyla needed this moment, needed to let it out.

When the sobs finally began to ease, Alexa spoke, her voice barely above a whisper. "How did you fall? Did you hit a pothole or something?"

It seemed to take all Kyla's strength to answer, "No... I just..."

Alexa didn't press. She stayed in the moment, watching the way Kyla's shoulders slumped under the weight of something heavier than a simple fall. This wasn't just about the tea bread incident—else was eating at her.

"You're exhausted," Alexa said gently, her worry deepening. "Let me take you home. I'll go get the car, okay?"

Before Alexa could move, Kyla staggered to her feet, barely making it before she doubled over and retched. She reached out instinctively, her hand steadying Kyla as she swayed.

"Oh, Kyla..." Alexa's voice was thick with worry as she gently rubbed her sister's back. "You're not okay, are you?"

Kyla wiped her mouth with the back of her hand and gave a weak nod. "I... I'm fine."

But Alexa knew better. As she hurried to her bike, a sense of hope took hold. Maybe this was the beginning—a small, fragile step toward healing, toward mending what had been broken.

*   *   *

As Alexa opened the car door, Kyla approached with slow, unsteady steps, her legs still trembling from the fall.

"Just sit here," Alexa said softly, guiding her toward the passenger seat. "I'll get your bike on the rack, then we'll go."

The warmth of the car enveloped Kyla as she sank into the seat, her body yielding to the softness of the cushions. It felt like a quiet release after the shock of the fall—her muscles finally unclenching in the safety of her sister's car. But more comforting than anything was the unspoken peace between her and Alexa. Kyla leaned her head back, letting that quiet settle in.

Alexa slid into the driver's seat and fastened her seatbelt with a soft click.

"So," she said lightly, "back to the commune, or maybe Cliffhouse?"

Kyla stared out the window, watching the fading light cast long shadows across the road. Her fingers traced slow, absent-minded circles on her thigh. The commune had been her haven, but now it felt tainted with memories of all that had gone wrong. The unease gnawed at her, churning her stomach. She thought of Jude—of how she'd probably never see him again—and the secret she carried, the one tugging her back toward Cliffhouse, where her true family had always welcomed her with open arms. Raine's betrayal only deepened her sense of isolation. What once felt like home now pressed down on her, too heavy to return to.

Kyla's voice came out small, almost lost. "You know, it's not that simple, Alexa. Things... they've changed. I've changed. And I'm not sure what to do anymore."

Kyla could feel Alexa's gaze—quiet, probing. She watched her sister shift forward slightly, fingers tightening around the steering wheel. Alexa was trying to understand, trying not to push.

"Oh, Kyla, can we just—" She let out a sigh, then her tone softened

"Okay, right now, I'm looking at my sister who needs a break. Let's get you home, get some food in you, and then you can decide what comes next. No pressure, okay?"

Kyla blinked, caught off guard by the invitation. Just an hour ago, their relationship had felt like it was splintering beyond repair—and now, Alexa was offering her a place to stay. After everything that had happened, after taking back the key, Alexa was opening the door again. It was a lifeline, a quiet glimmer of hope that maybe—just maybe—they could start to mend what had been broken.

But inside, Kyla's thoughts were in turmoil. She couldn't shake the whirlwind of emotions she hadn't sorted through—relief, guilt, anger— all crashing into her at once. It made her feel like she was barely holding it together, and she had to remind herself to breathe deeply to stave off the nausea still lurking. She didn't want to start retching again, not now, not with Alexa watching. She just needed to hold it together a little longer.

"I'm hungry," Kyla admitted, her voice barely holding steady. "If you're sure... I'd like to come home with you."

Alexa smiled, eyes warm with understanding. "You know me, Kyla. I wouldn't have offered if I didn't mean it."

As the engine hummed to life, Kyla leaned her head back against the seat and closed her eyes for a moment. And just for a second, in the quiet hum of the car and the steady rhythm of her sister's presence, something stirred—hope, fragile but real, rising like breath after too long under water.

Chapter Seventeen

Kyla stepped into the apartment behind Alexa, the familiar scent of lavender and lemon washing over her. Everything looked the same—the soft gray couch, the mismatched throw pillows—but it didn't feel the same. The air felt heavier somehow, dense with the weight of what had been lost between them.

Her gaze drifted to the small table near the door, where she had left her spare key just days ago. The memory surfaced instantly: Alexa's rigid stance, the silent tension as she held out her hand, waiting for Kyla to relinquish the key, and the crushing sense that she'd been shut out of her sister's life.

She swallowed hard, trying to suppress the emotions clawing their way up. But her body betrayed her.

"Alexa—" she choked, her voice catching as her hand brushed her sister's arm. Then she turned and bolted for the bathroom.

The door slammed behind her. Kyla barely made it to the sink before doubling over, her stomach lurching violently. The door slammed behind her. Kyla barely reached the sink before doubling over, her stomach lurching violently. The sounds of retching echoed off the tiled walls as she clung to the cold porcelain, breath ragged. The weight of it all—her mistakes, the widening gap between them, the secret growing inside her—pressed down, threatening to crush her.

She coughed, gasping for air between waves of nausea, then sank to the floor, her back pressed against the cool tile wall. The room tilted around her, and she shut her eyes, focusing on the rhythm of her breath. She felt humiliated, sitting there like a shattered version of herself.

A soft knock broke the silence.

"Kyla?" Alexa's voice came through the door, muffled but edged with concern. "Are you alright?"

Kyla opened her eyes and stared at the bathroom door, but said nothing. She couldn't face Alexa—not like this.

"I'm here if you need me," Alexa added, her voice calm but strained. The sound of it tugged at Kyla in a way she hadn't expected. It wasn't an offer filled with pity or judgment, but quiet reassurance.

Kyla hesitated before cracking the door open. Through the narrow gap, she saw Alexa standing a few steps back, worry etched across her face.

"I... I just need a moment," Kyla whispered, her voice barely audible.

She could feel Alexa's eyes on her, a mix of empathy and hesitation, as if waiting for permission to close the distance between them.

Alexa gave a slow nod and stepped back, respecting the fragile boundary. Kyla shut the door again, resting her head against the cool wall, willing herself to calm down. Moments later, she heard the soft clinking of something outside the door.

"I left some water and crackers for you," Alexa called gently.

Kyla cracked the door open just enough to see a glass of water and a plate of plain crackers sitting on a small wicker table. She managed a weak smile of gratitude, picking up the glass before closing the door again.

When Kyla finally emerged, still shaky but more composed, Alexa was waiting in the kitchen. She sat at the table, hands wrapped around a cup of tea, offering quiet patience instead of words. Kyla sat across from her, setting the untouched plate of crackers down.

"Tea?" Alexa asked, already moving to plug in the kettle.

Kyla nodded, still feeling unsteady but comforted by her sister's presence. Alexa moved about the kitchen, filling the kettle and retrieving another cup from the cupboard. They didn't need to speak—not yet. The ticking of the kitchen clock filled the silence as they sat together. Kyla nibbled on a cracker, not so much for sustenance, but to have something to do with her hands.

She glanced over at Alexa, who was quietly stirring her tea. The weight of everything still pressed down on Kyla—the mistakes, the secrets—but for the first time in what felt like forever, Kyla didn't feel like she had to carry it all alone. The distance between them was still there, but it felt a little less daunting, a little less impossible to bridge.

Maybe, just maybe, they could start finding their way back.

* * *

Considering Kyla's condition, Alexa decided not to press too hard about her troubles. Instead, she turned on some folk music, its gentle melodies filling the room as they sat together in quiet companionship. Outside, the setting sun cast a warm golden glow over the parking lot, a serene backdrop to their muted conversation.

After a while, Alexa glanced at Kyla, her expression thoughtful. "Hey, have you decided whether you want me to drop you at the commune, or would you prefer to go back home to Cliffhouse?"

Deep down, Alexa hoped Kyla would choose Cliffhouse. With the care of their loving mom, Jennie, and their cherished grandmother, Kathleen, Alexa had little doubt that Kyla would find her way back to herself in no time.

Alexa watched as Kyla's fork hovered mid-air, her gaze drifting to the window where the sunlight softened the edges of the world. The sight of Kyla, usually so confident and assured, showing even a hint of hesitation struck Alexa deeply.

Normally, Kyla would have objected to the idea of calling Cliffhouse her home after spending four years at EarthSong. But now, Alexa saw something different in her sister's eyes—an unsettled look, as if Kyla wasn't sure where she truly belonged anymore.

Maybe, deep down, she needs to be at Cliffhouse, Alexa thought, though she couldn't shake her own unease. She knew their mother would be shocked to see Kyla like this, but Jennie would likely give her daughter exactly what she needed right now.

Kyla's voice, small and hesitant, broke the silence. "Um, do you think I could borrow some clothes for work tomorrow, Lex?" Her tone was almost childlike, carrying a quiet vulnerability.

A wave of relief washed over Alexa. She could hear the unspoken choice in Kyla's request—the silent acceptance of Cliffhouse as a refuge in her time of need. "Don't worry, Kye. I'll pack a bag for you in case you want to stay for a few days," she said, offering a warm, reassuring smile.

Kyla sank back into her chair, a soft sigh slipping from her lips as she gazed out at the golden light. She hadn't fully articulated her decision, but in that moment, it felt a little easier to breathe.

Before heading to the bedroom, Alexa paused, watching her sister. The tension in Kyla's posture had eased—just slightly—but enough to give Alexa hope that she was starting to come back to herself.

Chapter Eighteen

At 7:00 p.m., Jennie waited while her mother, Kathleen, slipped into her cozy fleece pajamas and wrapped herself in a thick down comforter. With slow, deliberate movements, Kathleen made her way to the verandah and settled into the green settee, her eyes lifting to the starlit sky. Rollo padded out behind her, his tail swishing in lazy contentment.

Jennie followed her mother across the cool verandah floor, her bare feet making soft sounds against the wood. "Tea before bed, Mom?"

Kathleen chuckled, shaking her head. "Oh no, dear. I'd be up all night if I had tea now."

Jennie smiled as she watched Kathleen tuck the comforter snugly around her legs. Rollo curled up beside her on the floor, his head resting on his paws.

"I need to sort a few things for breakfast, Mom. Maybe Clay and I will join you in a bit."

Kathleen waved her hand dismissively, eyes fixed on the clear, starry night. "No rush, Jen. I could fall asleep right here."

A soft snort from Music, Jennie's palomino, was the only sound breaking the peaceful quiet. Rollo's tail thumped lazily against the floor, angling for more attention.

Jennie glanced at her mother and felt a deep, settling calm.

"Don't get too chilly out here," she said gently. "Let me know if you need another blanket."

"I'm warm as toast," Kathleen reassured with a smile, her voice low and content. "You know, Jen, I always sleep better after sitting out here a while."

Just then, the sound of tires crunching on the gravel driveway pierced the evening quiet. Rollo sprang up, bolting off the verandah and barking excitedly. Jennie squinted into the dim light and recognized Alexa's car. She called for Rollo to settle, but he was already wagging his tail wildly, excited to greet one of his favourite visitors.

"Well, there goes the peace," Kathleen said with a grin, craning her neck to catch a glimpse as the car pulled up near the kitchen door.

"Shattered," Jennie muttered, a slight frown crossing her face. "Strange for Alexa to drop by this late, especially on a Monday. I hope nothing's wrong."

She narrowed her eyes, peering closer. "Is that... Kyla?"

Jennie folded her arms against the evening chill, watching intently as Alexa stepped out, rounded the car, and opened the passenger door. Alexa's voice, muffled by distance, carried softly toward the verandah. "I'll get your bag, Kye," she said, stooping to rub Rollo's sides as he wiggled with excitement.

"Kyla?" Jennie called, stepping off the verandah as her daughter slowly emerged from the car. "What a lovely surprise."

It had been a week since Alexa's last visit, when she'd shared the unsettling story about the tea bread incident.

The initial shock had softened, but the worry lingered.

With Kyla's unexpected arrival, Jennie's joy was edged with concern.

Kyla managed a faint smile, but it lacked her usual spark. Jennie opened her arms and pulled her into an embrace, startled by how subdued her daughter felt, how her warmth seemed muted.

"Mom," Kyla murmured, her voice barely above a whisper, "I hope it's okay if I stay the night."

Jennie's heart sank, but she kept her tone steady and warm. "Of course, sweetheart. You know you're always welcome here."

She watched as Kyla's shoulders eased, just slightly—the tightness that had gripped her frame beginning to soften. Nearby, Alexa—ever the one to smooth the rough edges—hoisted the overnight bag and set it on the verandah steps before crossing over to Kathleen, wearing the calm, reassuring smile that always made Jennie feel steadier in moments like this.

"Sorry to bother you, Grandma," Alexa said gently. "I know it's close to bedtime."

Kathleen chuckled, sitting up and spreading her arms wide to pull Alexa into a hug. Jennie couldn't help but smile at the sight, her heart lightening as she watched the loving exchange.

"Oh, hush," Kathleen said, pressing a kiss to her granddaughter's cheek. "Now, where's my favourite hippie?"

Jennie's heart warmed as Kyla knelt beside the settee, leaning in to kiss her grandmother.

"Hi, Grandma," Kyla whispered with a faint smile. "I hope we're not keeping you up."

Rollo, eager for his share of attention, wedged himself between the two sisters, earning a gentle scratch behind his ears from Kyla. Jennie watched her daughter's hands move through the familiar motion, a brief moment of comfort amid the unspoken tension.

The screen door creaked open, and Clay stepped out, beer in hand. His brow furrowed as he took in the scene. "What's this?" he asked, concern lacing his voice. "Everything okay?"

Alexa quickly stepped in. "Oh, everything's fine, Clay. Kyla's just staying here for the night. She was at my apartment, and I figured I'd drive her over."

Jennie caught the subtle shift in Clay's expression as he processed the information, his concern softening but still present. She appreciated Alexa's calm approach, but couldn't shake her nagging worry. Something about Kyla's sudden appearance gnawed at her, though she didn't want to press—yet.

Clay nodded slowly. "Alright, then. Nice to see you both," he said with a welcoming smile.

Jennie watched as Kyla swiftly grabbed the overnight bag and headed into the house. "I'll get settled in my room, Mom, if that's okay," she called over her shoulder.

Jennie's gaze lingered on Kyla's retreating figure, the entryway light accentuating her scraped skin and weary eyes. A wave of concern surged within Jennie, but instead of probing, she stepped forward and gently touched Kyla's shoulder. "There are leftovers in the kitchen if you're hungry."

Kyla's face brightened, if only for a moment. "I'd love that. Do you have any ginger tea? And maybe some cheese for a grilled cheese sandwich?"

Jennie smiled warmly. "I've got everything you need. Go ahead and get settled, and I'll fix it for you."

"Thanks, Mom," Kyla said, her voice laced with relief as she disappeared up the familiar staircase.

Jennie watched her daughter go, the weight of unspoken concerns settling over her like the cool night air.

* * *

In the quiet of her childhood bedroom, Kyla knelt beside the bed, her fingers brushing the worn zipper of Alexa's overnight bag. The familiar fragrance of her sister's lavender lotion wafted up as she unzipped it, and she couldn't help but smile. She pulled out the neatly folded clothes—three full sets, enough for a few days' stay.

As her hands grazed the soft fabric, a wave of warmth spread through her. Alexa had packed everything she might need, down to the small toiletry bag, thoughtfully tucked into the side pocket. Kyla paused, her heart swelling with a deep sense of gratitude. It wasn't just the clothes or the bag, but the unspoken understanding between them. She smiled to herself, her heart brimming with love for her twin, and grateful that Cliffhouse was always there for the good times, the bad times, and everything in between.

Kyla glanced out the window, the soft glow of the moon casting shadows over the garden below, and she let out a quiet breath. She was home.

Chapter Nineteen

Kyla crawled under the covers, sinking into the familiar softness of the bed. The sheets were cool, the pillow perfectly cradling her head. She exhaled, feeling the comfort that came from being at Cliffhouse. But as the minutes passed, her body grew restless, legs tangling in the sheets. She turned to one side, then the other, unable to sleep.

At 3:25 a.m., her eyes flew open, her heart pounding, a wave of panic rushing through her. *Not pregnant*—the thought jolted through her, and for a second, she believed it. But as her breath steadied and the fog of sleep cleared, the truth crept back in. She pressed a hand to her lower abdomen, where she believed a new life, faint but certain, had begun. The positive test lingered in her memory, as undeniable as the steady pulse of her heartbeat.

Kyla decided not to tell her family until she had confirmation from Dr. Shelley. *Raine, don't you dare tell anyone.* Her brow furrowed, and she pushed the thought away, along with the weight of EarthSong, not ready to face any of it.

She slid out of bed, the wooden floor cold against her feet. In the bathroom, the faucet creaked as she splashed water on her face, the coolness grounding her. A small sip from the glass on the sink soothed her dry throat. Back in bed, she pulled the blanket tight, cocooning herself as she had as a child, hoping it would offer the same comfort. Soon, sleep took her.

It wasn't the rooster crowing at sunrise that woke her, but her phone's alarm at seven a.m. She silenced it and lay back, not ready to face the day. Her thoughts drifted to Alexa and the deep loss that lingered between them. In the past, Alexa would have been the first person she confided in, even when she couldn't tell anyone else. They'd always shared secrets, from the time they were little.

She could almost hear the echo of Alexa's voice, the way they used to talk about everything—fears, dreams, secrets that no one else would ever know. Their midnight talks on the roof, under a blanket of stars, felt like another lifetime. They'd laughed through tears, making promises to always be there for each other, through heartbreaks, through every trial. But now, Kyla faced the uncertainty on her own.

Lying in bed, with the scent of morning coffee in the air, Kyla felt the weight of Alexa's absence more than ever. What once was a comforting aroma now felt like a cruel reminder of mornings spent together, planning their futures and supporting each other against the world. She longed for the days when Alexa was just a call away, ready to share a secret or offer a shoulder to cry on. The world felt colder and lonelier, without her twin by her side.

A beam of sunlight streaked across the bedroom, highlighting the warm woodgrain floor. Kyla forced herself up and peeked out the small hexagonal window, spotting Clay busy with his morning chores, Rollo trotting close behind.

Kyla dressed quickly, pulling on her clinic clothes—grey

jeans and a black long-sleeved top. The familiar fabric wrapped her in a layer of protection, as if wearing her sister's clothes could shield her from the chaos still spinning in her mind.

Downstairs, the kitchen hummed with life. Kathleen stood by the stove, the rhythmic clatter of dishes filling the air. The smell of fresh coffee mingled with the sweet scent of vanilla, and Kyla guessed what was baking. *Probably Grandma's famous vanilla scones,* Kyla thought—a treat that always brought warmth and nostalgia. The scents wrapped around her like a comforting embrace, momentarily easing the ache in her heart.

"Good morning, dear," Kathleen greeted cheerfully. "Did you sleep well?"

Kyla forced a small smile, wanting to please her grandmother. "Like a baby."

"I made some oatmeal. Would you like some?"

"That sounds perfect, Grandma," Kyla replied, moving toward the stove to scoop some into a bowl. She sat at the table, the steam from the porridge rising lazily as she poured milk into the small wells she made with her spoon, cooling it off just like she had as a child.

As she raised the first spoonful to her lips, Kathleen suddenly clapped a hand to her forehead. "Oh, what was I thinking? I forgot the raspberries."

She bustled to the fridge, pulling out a glass bowl filled with last summer's raspberries, their rich scent filling the room as she stirred them with a spoon.

The moment the aroma hit Kyla, her stomach twisted violently. The sweetness, once a cherished memory, now turned her insides. She dropped the spoon with a clatter, the chair legs scraping against the floor as she bolted for the bathroom, hand clamped over her mouth, barely making it in time.

Chapter Twenty

Kyla had spent three nights at Cliffhouse, but the thought of asking her mother for rides to and from work, like she did as a teenager, made her uneasy. However, right now she had no other choice. She had asked Jennie to drive her back to EarthSong instead of returning to Cliffhouse after work on Wednesday. She had an appointment with Dr. Shelley at eight o'clock on Thursday morning—a secret she kept from Jennie. The last thing she wanted was for her mother to drop her off and wait around at that appointment.

As Kyla retrieved Alexa's overnight bag from the back seat, Jennie's voice broke the silence. "Kyla, you know you're welcome to stay at the farm anytime, right?" Her tone was gentle, but Kyla could sense the underlying concern.

"Yes, Mom," Kyla replied, smiling. I think we all know that our Mama Bear is there for us at all times." She walked around to the driver's side window and leaned in to kiss Jennie on the cheek.

"What about dinner on Sunday, dear? Would that work for

you?" Jennie asked without waiting for an answer before adding, "Your grandmother is counting on it. She plans to bake your favourite cake for dessert... devil's food. As opposed to Nick's favourite, angel food."

Kyla chuckled, stepping back and giving her mother a quick wave goodbye. "How could I possibly resist an invitation like that, Mom?"

* * *

The overnight bag felt heavier in Kyla's grip as she climbed the steps to EarthSong. This time, something was different. The familiar creak of the wooden steps didn't bring the same sense of comfort. Instead, a heaviness seemed to drag her down—she was leaving behind the place that now felt like home. A pull deep inside her longed to turn around, to go back to Cliffhouse, where her heart had truly settled.

The door swung open, and she was greeted by Raine, grinning widely. "Kyla, where've you been? We looked for you at Eve's birthday last night."

Kyla blinked, caught off guard. *Eve's birthday.* She had completely forgotten. Normally, those celebrations were marked by small, meaningful gestures—a wildflower bouquet, a song, a massage. But last night, she'd been wrapped in a blanket of warmth, sitting on the Cliffhouse verandah, surrounded by the people who mattered most. No comparison. Her family was rare and precious, a bond she couldn't imagine breaking.

"Oh," she said, her voice soft, "I forgot about Eve's birthday." She shifted her bag on her shoulder, trying to sound casual. "I was just home visiting my family for a few days."

Raine's grin only widened. "Did you tell them?"

Kyla's stomach tightened, a knot forming. "Tell them what?"

"You know." Raine's eyes sparkled, her excitement almost offensive. "About the little person growing inside your belly."

The words hit like a slap. Kyla stiffened, her jaw clenching. She hadn't even fully processed the possibility herself, and here was Raine, so carefree and bold about something so personal. She forced herself to breathe, her lips pressing into a thin line. "Raine," she said, her voice tight, "I wish you wouldn't talk about that. It's not confirmed. And I hope you haven't told anyone else."

Raine's eyebrows shot up, her hands flitting in the air as if to brush the tension away. "No worries, Sundance. Your secret's safe with me." Then, as if Kyla hadn't just set a boundary, Raine added, "By the way, who's the father?"

Heat crept up Kyla's neck. She gripped the bag tighter, fighting the urge to snap. "I don't know, and I don't even know if I'm pregnant. Can we drop it?"

Raine's carefree demeanor didn't waver. "Okay, okay. But let me know when you find out for sure, 'kay?" With a breezy wave, she skipped down the stairs toward the bike rack, leaving Kyla standing there, simmering.

Inside her room, Kyla tossed the bag down, her mind still spinning from the encounter. She forced herself into action, gathering Alexa's clothes and tossing them into the washing machine. She needed the distraction. Tomorrow's appointment with Dr. Shelley loomed, and her nerves hummed with the weight of what might come next.

As she passed the chore wheel on her way to the kitchen, a flicker of guilt surfaced. She hadn't chosen her task for the week. Normally, it would've bothered her more, but right now, her priorities felt different. She had bigger things to deal with.

The sound of chatter and clattering dishes filled the kitchen area, and for a moment, Kyla let herself smile. *Pasta night. Comfort food.* She approached the serving table, grabbing a bowl and helping herself to a modest portion of noodles. As she reached for the pesto sauce, a gentle touch on her arm startled her.

"Kyla," Lily's soft voice came from behind. "I hear you have good news."

Kyla stopped short, her heart skipping a beat. *Surely, she doesn't mean the pregnancy.*

Kyla's heart skipped, a cold wave of dread washing over her. She froze, carefully setting the pasta claw down before turning to face Lily. "Good news?" Her voice was steady, but inside, she braced herself. *Surely she didn't mean...*

Lily smiled, her eyes twinkling with unspoken understanding. "Don't worry, your secret's safe with me."

Kyla felt a surge of frustration, but she kept her expression neutral, forcing a tight smile. "I'm just happy it's pasta night. Basil pesto is my favourite." She turned her focus back to the meal, letting Lily's chatter fade into the background, her mind churning with a mixture of irritation and exhaustion.

Chapter Twenty-One

At 8:00 a.m. on Thursday, Kyla stepped into the tiny examination room, greeted by Dr. Shelley's warm smile. The room felt both familiar and comforting, a small haven amid her swirling thoughts. Dr. Shelley, with her kind eyes and reassuring presence, had been a constant in Kyla's life for as long as she could remember. Despite the professional setting, she always managed to make Kyla feel like she was chatting with an old friend.

"Even though you got a positive result on your home pregnancy test," Dr. Shelley said, her voice steady and calm, "we'll do both urine and blood tests today to confirm that result."

Kyla nodded, the words washing over her like a gentle wave. The clinic, with its sterile yet somehow welcoming atmosphere, was a place where she felt safe. Dr. Shelley had known her family for decades, yet she managed to be non-judgmental, a quality that eased Kyla's anxious mind and instilled trust.

"I'll check your blood pressure and do a pelvic examination, all standard stuff," Dr. Shelley continued, her tone reassuring. "And we'll have your test results in six to eight days."

Kyla took a deep breath, feeling a mix of anticipation and gratitude. The familiarity of the routine, the kindness in Dr. Shelley's eyes, and the promise of answers soon felt like an anchor in a sea of uncertainty.

* * *

By the time Kyla rushed into the vet clinic at 9:30 a.m., she felt the weight of her tardiness. "I'm sorry, Dr. Nicholls," she said, panting, her cheeks flushing with embarrassment. "The appointment took longer than I thought. I hope my absence didn't put you too far behind."

To her surprise, Dr. Nicholls smiled—a warm, genuine smile that she wasn't used to seeing from him. "We're running a bit late, but nothing I can't handle," he said, his tone light. Then, he winked at her. *A wink?* Kyla's mind raced. *That was definitely out of character.*

She quickly looked away, trying to process the unexpected gesture. *What's going on?* She felt a jolt of uncertainty, a sharp disruption in her usually steady routine.

"Ah, okay," she managed to say, striving to keep her voice steady. "I'd better get to it then." She slipped behind the reception desk, her fingers flying over the keyboard as she checked the schedule. "Fiona, please bring Marcus into Treatment Room 3," she called out, her voice regaining its usual confidence. "I'll get you set up in there, and Dr. Nicholls will be in soon."

As she moved through the familiar motions, Kyla couldn't shake the feeling that something had shifted. Dr. Nicholls' wink lingered in her mind. The familiar rhythm of her day now felt off-kilter, the unsettling gesture puzzling.

* * *

Friday, at the end of the workday, Kyla tidied up the front desk, intending to head back to EarthSong, but found herself struggling to move forward. She felt exhausted and weighed down by her thoughts. Gone were the days of sharing the excitement of an upcoming weekend with Alexa as they biked home together. Normally, Kyla would have been eager to tell Alexa about the weekend activities planned at EarthSong—especially the felting workshop this weekend—but her mind was clouded with heavy concerns.

Do I want to keep living at EarthSong now that I'm probably pregnant? Would I want to stay there anyway, now that I feel differently about Raine? The questions circled in her mind, creating a tight knot of uncertainty. These were things she would have talked through with Alexa, staying up late until they hashed out a plan of action that made sense. Kyla valued her sister's opinion, but now there were too many secrets she couldn't share. The void between them seemed to widen with each passing day, and Kyla couldn't shake the feeling of being alone in a storm without a compass.

Kyla's thoughts drifted to the night with Jude, a tangled mix of emotions she couldn't even begin to unravel. *I might just as well forget about Jude. What good could come of my trying to find him? What do I expect of him, anyway?* This wasn't how she'd ever imagined starting a family. Alexa had a way of cutting through the chaos, helping Kyla see what truly mattered and guiding her toward a sensible solution. But on her own, Kyla felt like a boat set adrift, scared of what was to come and uncertain of how to navigate it all.

With a heavy heart, Kyla gathered her handbag and jacket, feeling more unsettled than ever. She placed her hand on the doorknob, ready to leave the clinic and breathe in the fresh, crisp air that she hoped would clear her mind.

"Oh, Kyla, could we chat for a moment, please?"

Kyla paused, a heaviness settling in. A chat was the last thing she wanted right now. She wasn't in the mood for Earth-Song, either. All she craved was a little solitude and the soothing rhythm of her bike ride home.

Twisting her body toward Dr. Nicholls while still holding the doorknob, Kyla forced a small smile. "Yes?" she replied, trying to keep the agitation out of her voice.

Dr. Nicholls had changed into his street clothes, ready to leave the clinic. "I just wanted to wish you a good weekend," he said, sounding tentative, but Kyla sensed there was more he wanted to say.

"Thanks. Same to you," Kyla replied, her grip tightening on the doorknob. She offered a quick nod before turning away, leaving him to close the clinic on his own.

Chapter Twenty-Two

By Sunday, Alexa noticed that Kyla seemed restless, almost like she was looking for an excuse to get away from EarthSong. When their grandmother Kathleen extended a dinner invitation, Alexa sensed Kyla's eagerness—it was as if the invitation was exactly what Kyla needed.

Alexa watched as her sister descended the steps of Earth-Song, a smile on her face. Alexa had never set foot in the ecovillage before today, a fact that hadn't seemed important at the time. She knew their mother and grandmother would never visit, dismissing EarthSong as a place full of 'hippies,' but she realized now how her absence might have hurt Kyla. As Kyla climbed into Alexa's red Toyota Corolla, Alexa couldn't help but imagine her sister was stepping into a royal carriage, eager to be whisked away from whatever burdens she carried at EarthSong. When Kyla fastened her seatbelt and exhaled, Alexa caught the subtle sigh and wondered what was going through her sister's mind.

"What's that about, my dear?" Alexa teased, glancing sideways at her.

Kyla let out a light laugh. "Oh," she said, "I guess that's my way of saying I'm relieved to be here with you, Alexa. Honestly, it feels good to get away from EarthSong."

Alexa felt a warm rush of satisfaction. It was clear that Kyla was genuinely enjoying the break, and Alexa was pleased to be the one providing it.

As they drove towards Cliffhouse, Alexa glanced over and asked with a teasing lilt, "Hmmm, do I detect a change of heart, Kyla?" She kept her tone light, careful not to sound too eager.

Kyla paused, and Alexa noticed the hesitation. "I can't fool you, Alexa. I admit I'm having second thoughts."

Alexa's heart lifted at the admission.

"Well, you know, Kye, those words are music to my ears." She gave a playful grin. "What would be even more musical—and magical," she laughed, "is if you told me you were moving out."

Kyla sighed, and Alexa picked up on the frustration in her voice. "I'm working on it, Alexa, but these things take time. Can you imagine uprooting yourself from Grace Square, where you've lived for, what, five years now?"

"No," Alexa replied without missing a beat, "but that's because I love it there. Sounds like your heart's no longer in the ecovillage."

"Things change," Kyla said with a shrug.

Alexa sensed there was more she wasn't saying, and it stung. They used to share everything—from their biggest dreams to their smallest secrets. She missed those long nights of hashing things out until it all made sense.

"They sure do," Alexa said softly, her voice carrying the weight of the distance between them. She didn't want to push. There'd be time to mend things, just... not tonight. Kyla seemed too raw, and Alexa didn't want to spoil the evening.

Kyla changed the subject, saying, "I can't wait to see Nick again. I think he's coming on the 16th."

Alexa perked up. It had been a while since she'd seen her brother, and the thought of his visit added an extra note of excitement to weeks ahead.

"That's right," she said. "Just before the Christmas market. I wonder what Emily's like."

"I don't know, Lex, but Mom says Nick's smitten."

"Yeah. Remember how miserable he was in undergrad? I think he threatened to quit every week," Alexa said.

"And then not a word of complaint once he met Emily and they enrolled in chiropractic college," said Kyla.

"So, was it Emily that made all the difference, or chiropractic?" Alexa asked.

"Guess we'll find out," Kyla said.

As Alexa's reliable red Toyota pulled into the driveway at Cliffhouse, she glanced over at Kyla and noticed her sister's gaze lingering on their childhood home. The decorative verandah always stood out as always, a symbol of countless memories. Alexa felt a wave of nostalgia, laced with quiet gratitude.

Rollo's excited barking echoed as they approached, and Alexa smiled, warmed by the familiar sounds of home.

Kyla's voice was soft but sure. "You know, Lexi, this will always be our home no matter where we go or what life throws at us."

Alexa nodded, her heart swelling at the truth of it. The words wrapped around her like a comforting embrace, reminding her of the deep connection they shared and the enduring significance of their childhood home.

"It's true, Kye. We're so lucky to have this place, and Mom and Grandma made sure the farm would stay in the family as long as possible. It's like an anchor—something that keeps us grounded, no matter what."

Chapter Twenty-Three

Kyla glanced at the two-layer devil's food cake perched on a glass pedestal cake plate. She smiled. "Grandma, you're the best," she said, her tone reflecting genuine appreciation.

The lively and warm atmosphere at dinner felt like a world away from the tension of just two weeks ago. Jennie and Kathleen seemed at ease, their concern about the twins' relationship appearing to have faded. As Rollo snapped up a fallen scrap of roast beef, Clay's voice drew Kyla's attention.

"You might have met him when he visited me here on Sunrise in 2019," Clay said. "I was still renting the farmhouse on Arbutus Lane."

Kyla listened as Alexa responded playfully, "I do indeed recall a tall, handsome young man, a clone of his dad, stepping up to the verandah one fine summer's day." She noticed Clay's pleased smile and felt a twinge of curiosity. She remained quiet, her thoughts shifting to the possibility of Patrick moving to the island.

"Patrick is 22 now and dying to get out of Dublin," Clay

continued. "He's like me... craves the countryside and loves the wide, open spaces of BC. He's interested in helping me with my paragliding business."

Kyla's mind spun. What would it mean to have Patrick living next door? Where would he stay? Her thoughts were interrupted by Alexa's enthusiastic comment: "A budding Clay, for sure."

Kyla asked, "What has he been doing in Dublin?"

"Since he graduated from high school," Clay replied, "he's been working in construction, so his skills are portable."

"I'm sure we could put those skills to use right here at Cliffhouse," Alexa said, her excitement unmistakable. Kyla could feel it too, but hers was laced with apprehension.

Kathleen's voice cut through Kyla's thoughts, "We'd welcome your son with open arms. And I'm sure he could stay here, at least until he gets settled, Jennie, isn't that right?"

Kyla watched Jennie nod. "Yes, Clay and I have been talking about renting out the two side-by-side houses that used to be the B&B."

Kyla's thoughts tumbled. The idea of Patrick living in one of those houses jarred her, especially when she'd long imagined raising her baby there herself.

She nearly choked on her chocolate cake. Taking a sip of water, she cleared her throat, excused herself, and pushed back her chair. "Sorry, Grandma's cake is so tasty, I think I was a bit greedy there for a moment. I'll be right back."

Kyla headed into the kitchen and opened the screen door. Her thoughts swirled as she tried to absorb what she'd just heard. Stepping outside, she looked toward the two side-by-side houses. She had always pictured herself living in one of them, building a life at Cliffhouse with her baby, close to family. Now, that vision felt suddenly threatened.

As she stood there, Kyla sensed Jennie watching her. The

concern on her mother's face was unmistakable. As she stepped into the damp evening air, the familiar scent of hay filled her lungs. Jennie followed her out, the barn's rustic aroma mingling with the cool night air.

"Kyla," Jennie began gently, "I was thinking... you might want to move into one of those units yourself."

Kyla turned, managing a smile. "Ha, Mom. You must be a mind-reader."

"What do you mean, dear? Have you already thought of moving back to the farm?"

"More and more every day." *It would be a wonderful place to raise my baby—close to family, with room to grow.*

"Kyla, why didn't you say so? I've been toying with the idea of suggesting it, but I didn't want to push. I know how much you value your life at EarthSong..."

"Not so much, Mom. Things have changed."

"It's in ready-to-move-in condition, dear. Want to take a look?"

Once inside the unit, Kyla had a good look around. She turned to Jennie, her excitement obvious.

"Mom, I can't tell you how excited I am about moving here. If you can help me move my few possessions back to the farm, I'd like to start as soon as possible. If not sooner," she added with a laugh.

Jennie smiled, then shifted gears.

"Clay and I were talking last night, and we agreed—if you want to leave your job at the vet clinic and work here on the farm instead, we could find enough paid work for you. You know we like to keep things in the family, and there's so much potential here."

"I know, Mom. There's the campsite idea, the cabin rentals, the sheep, the farmstand, the organic produce—it never ends."

"You could always switch things up later if you wanted. But we'd love to give you the option if it feels right."

"That would cut down on my commute," Kyla said with a chuckle, though the idea of leaving Dr. Nicholls gave her pause. She wasn't sure why it felt complicated.

"If you don't mind, I need some time to think it over. Things have been pretty rough at work lately, so the idea of leaving sounds appealing." It was the kind of decision she used to hash out with Alexa, but things still felt unsettled between them. And this—this felt too heavy to lay on her sister just yet.

Chapter Twenty-Four

After Sunday supper at Cliffhouse, Kyla offered to help with the cleanup, but Jennie gently waved her off with a smile that warmed Kyla's heart.

"No, dear," Jennie said kindly, "just enjoy yourself. We don't get to see you very often these days—go relax and soak in the beauty of the farm."

Kyla nodded, though a trace of unease from the evening still lingered in her stomach.

"Thanks, Mom. I think I'll take a walk through the orchards —maybe head up to the clifftop."

She turned to her grandmother and wrapped her in a warm hug, planting a kiss on her cheek.

"Grandma, thank you so much. I loved the devil's food cake —just like you knew I would. You're so thoughtful. I love you to bits."

Kyla felt a deep comfort in her grandmother's smile as Kathleen's face lit up.

"Sweetheart, it's my pleasure. I just wish you'd come by more often," Kathleen said, holding Kyla close.

Kyla managed a smile. "I'm going to catch some of that fresh clifftop air before we head out, Grandma. I'll be back soon."

She zipped up her jacket against the cool breeze and set off toward the clifftop, hoping the walk would help clear her head. But before long, she heard footsteps swishing through the long grass behind her.

"Hey, Kyla—do you want to be alone?" Alexa called, slightly out of breath as she hurried to catch up. "It's totally fine if you do," she added, though Kyla could hear the hope in her voice.

Kyla glanced back, a smile tugging at the corners of her mouth despite the heaviness she felt.

"Oh no, it's all good. Please—come. Just like old times, sis."

They walked side by side, the path well-worn and familiar beneath their feet, until they reached the clifftop. Kyla crossed her arms against the chill, her eyes fixed on the restless sea.

Alexa's voice gently broke the silence. "You seemed quiet after dessert. Is something going on?"

Kyla blinked rapidly, trying to hold back the tears, but her emotions were too raw to hide.

"To tell you the truth, Alexa, I was thinking of asking Mom if I could move into one of the side-by-sides," she said, her voice unsteady as she looked down, embarrassed by her own vulner-ability.

Alexa didn't hesitate.

"Kyla, I was going to suggest the same thing," she said, her warmth and enthusiasm wrapping around Kyla like a hug. "I think it's perfect timing."

"What do you mean?" Kyla asked, brushing away a tear that had slipped down her cheek.

"The houses have been empty for two years, and Mom and Clay have been talking about renting them out. What could be better than you living back on the farm? The whole place will eventually be ours anyway."

Kyla felt a quiet sense of hope take root, encouraged by her sister's support.

"But what about Patrick?" she asked, anxiety tightening in her stomach.

"What about him?" Alexa said with a casual shrug, her tone surprisingly reassuring. "He's Clay's son, and from what I remember, he's a nice guy. Wouldn't you rather have someone like that next door than a complete stranger?"

Kyla took a long, steady breath, letting the cool sea air fill her lungs before releasing it slowly.

"Yeah, I see what you mean, Lexi. I don't know why I'm so nervous about it."

But deep down, she knew exactly why. She could feel the weight of her secret, the uncertainty gnawing at her. She wasn't ready to share her pregnancy news—not until it was confirmed by Dr. Shelley. And Kyla found herself seeking more encouragement to take the next step, especially from Alexa.

Alexa reached out, her touch brief but reassuring. "It seems to me you've had a change of heart toward EarthSong... am I right?"

Kyla smiled softly. "I can't hide much from my twin, can I?" she said, teasing lightly. "But you're right. I've been there for four years now, and I feel it's time to move on."

Move forward, Kyla thought, letting her sister's words echo in her mind.

"It's important to listen to your heart," Alexa said gently. "Shall we head back and let Mom know what we're thinking?"

Kyla nodded, the decision beginning to feel solid.

"Mom already offered to let me live in one of the units, Lex. I'm going to move in as soon as possible."

Alexa lit up. She didn't let Kyla's careful tone dampen her enthusiasm.

"Which house are you leaning toward, Kye?" Before Kyla could answer, Alexa added quickly, "I'd go for the one attached to the breezeway. No need to cross the yard when it's raining. Plus, it's got a better view of the ocean."

Kyla followed her gaze toward the rental units and smiled. She'd already chosen that one in her mind the moment they drove up the driveway for supper.

"Yes," she said, more sure now. "I can't wait to move in."

Chapter Twenty-Five

The next day at the vet clinic passed in a blur as Kyla moved through her tasks on autopilot, her thoughts drifting often to the idea of living at Cliffhouse again.

Back at EarthSong, she kept mostly to herself, sidestepping small talk with friends. After work, she took a long walk, letting the cool air settle her nerves. A light snack helped ease the morning nausea, and she turned in early, retreating to the quiet of her room.

On Friday morning, right at 8:00 a.m., her phone buzzed.

"Kyla, this is Dr. Shelley. I have the results of your pregnancy tests."

Kyla's heart pounded. She pressed the phone tighter to her ear, trying to steady her voice.

"Good morning, Dr. Shelley. Yes, please—go ahead."

She held her breath, waiting.

"The tests were positive," Dr. Shelley said. "You're about eight weeks along. That gives you a due date of July 12."

A mix of relief and reality settled over Kyla. She'd suspected it, but hearing the confirmation made it feel undeniably real. A wave of emotions surged—anticipation, fear, something like awe.

"Okay," she said, trying to sound composed. "That's good to know, Dr. Shelley. Thanks for calling."

Just as she was about to end the call, Dr. Shelley's voice gently cut in.

"And how are you feeling about the pregnancy?"

Kyla sighed and glanced at the clock, as if it might offer the right answer.

"Well... you know I'm single, so... there's that."

"That can make things more challenging, no question," Dr. Shelley replied. "But let's talk more at your next visit. I'll have Reception call you to schedule a few appointments—it's standard for all new mothers."

All new mothers.

Kyla swallowed hard, still trying to wrap her mind around being part of that group.

* * *

By the time she woke the next morning, Kyla felt more certain than she had in weeks—it was time for a change. With the pregnancy confirmed, moving out of the ecovillage felt not just necessary but inevitable. The lingering shame from the vaccine mix-up at the clinic only solidified her decision. She didn't need the added stress of Dr. Nicholls' unpredictable moods on top of everything else.

After her shift, Kyla approached him, feeling nervous but determined. His face, typically so composed, registered visible surprise when she told him she'd be leaving the clinic as soon as her contract allowed. She softened her tone, hoping to ease the moment.

"I don't want to leave you in a lurch, Dr. Nicholls," she

said. "I'm happy to train whoever you hire over the next two weeks."

"Yes," he said, looking away. "That's the usual procedure." His voice was clipped, and Kyla couldn't tell whether he was annoyed or just taking in the news.

"Is there a particular reason you're leaving, Kyla?" he asked after a pause, finally meeting her gaze.

She hesitated, choosing her words with care.

"I'm moving back to the family farm to help out," she said, then paused, debating whether to say more. "...and to raise my baby."

Something passed over Dr. Nicholls' face—too quick to name—but it left her unsettled.

"I see," he said quietly. After a moment, he added, almost to himself, "Perhaps that explains a few things."

Kyla wasn't in the mood for a deeper conversation. She offered a polite smile, keeping things light.

"I'll keep an eye out for a replacement, Dr. Nicholls," she said, injecting as much warmth into her voice as she could.

As she pedaled back to EarthSong, a pang of sadness caught her off guard. She'd worked beside him for four years. Despite the challenges, part of her knew—she'd miss him.

Chapter Twenty-Six

Friday, Late Morning

Jennie and Bev continued preparing for the market. The paper products still hadn't arrived. They'd set traps and brought in Bev's cat to try to address the rodent problem, which had been detected by droppings under one of the display tables. Bev and Jennie were thorough. Their new mission was to check under and over all the tables and corners of the building every single day until the problem was resolved.

At 11:30, Jennie's phone chimed, displaying Kyla's name.

"Kyla, good morning. How nice to hear from you," Jennie answered, her voice warm. "How are things?"

"Good, Mom," Kyla replied cordially. "Listen, I was wondering if you could meet me on the dock outside the Sunrise Café around noon." She spoke quickly, barely pausing for a breath. "I won't have much time... have to leave by 12:45. But I'll pick up a couple of coffees, and maybe we could chat briefly. Would that work for you?"

"Oh," Jennie replied, sounding surprised by the sudden

invitation. "Well, sure. That sounds like a nice break in my day, dear. I'll see you soon."

* * *

Kyla pulled her bike up to the café and spotted Jennie sitting on the dock bench, two take-out cups in hand. Kyla's stomach tightened as she realized the time had come to share news she hadn't fully processed herself.

"Aw, thanks, Mom. You're way ahead of me," she said, accepting the coffee Jennie offered.

"What's up, sweetie?" Jennie asked, sipping her drink, her voice warm and familiar.

Kyla took a breath, her thoughts racing as she gazed out at the boats bobbing in the marina. She felt the urge to blurt it all out, but the words caught in her throat. "A couple of things, Mom," she began, trying to sound casual but knowing the weight of what she was about to reveal. She could feel Jennie's full attention on her, the way her mother's body language reflected her readiness to listen.

"First of all, I wanted to let you know that I'm really happy with my decision to leave EarthSong..."

Kyla saw the subtle shift in Jennie's expression—a smile, gentle but reserved, as if she were bracing herself for whatever came next.

"You look just like your dear father right now, Kyla," Jennie said warmly. "Derrick would have been so proud of you and Alexa, had he lived this long." Her voice softened, but Kyla could hear the undertone of longing. "We'd love to have you back at Cliffhouse. And the units are separate enough from the main house that you'd have as much privacy as you'd want."

But as Kyla listened to her mother's words, an unwelcome

nervousness crept in. She shifted uncomfortably on the bench, then stood up, pacing a few steps on the dock before returning.

Kyla nodded, trying to absorb her mother's words, but a knot of unease tightened in her stomach. She shifted on the bench, her mind racing with the bigger news she still had to share. She stood up, pacing a few steps along the dock before turning back to face Jennie. Her mother's expectant gaze followed her, and the weight of her unspoken words pressed heavily against Kyla.

"I agree, Mom, I think the unit attached to the breezeway would be perfect for me, especially considering my circumstances," Kyla said, her voice steadying as she met Jennie's eyes.

As Jennie continued, Kyla's patience wore thin. "Yes," said Jennie, "it's timely that you've decided to leave the commune just as Clay and I've decided to rent the two units. The timing couldn't be better," Jennie added, her tone bright. "Imagine if we'd already rented them before you asked."

Kyla forced a smile, but the rapid beat of her heart betrayed her. She had to say it, no matter how much she dreaded the impact it would have. "I know, Mom, but I have some bigger news that I'm finding difficult to say... because I know you won't be happy when you hear it."

As she spoke, Kyla saw Jennie's expression shift, the colour draining from her face as concern took hold. Jennie reached out, her hand resting gently on Kyla's—a familiar gesture meant to comfort. But instead of easing her nerves, the touch only heightened Kyla's anxiety, the tension in her chest growing tighter.

"What is it, dear?" Jennie's voice was soft, but Kyla could feel the shift in the air, the tension rising between them.

Kyla took a deep breath, the words tumbling out before she could stop them. "I'm pregnant."

The confession hung heavy in the air, the sounds of the

bustling café and the distant cries of seagulls fading into a thick silence. Jennie's hand slid away, and Kyla felt a chill spread through her, the warmth of the sun no longer reaching her.

"I... I don't know what to say, dear," Jennie stammered, her voice faint, her eyes searching Kyla's face. The confusion and concern were evident, unspoken questions hanging between them. "Was it planned?"

Kyla shook her head, her voice barely a whisper. "No, Mom. It wasn't planned. I'm too young to be a mother. Not that I never wanted kids... but I never imagined I'd be pregnant at twenty-two." She wrung her hands, fighting the tears that threatened to spill. She couldn't let them complicate things further.

Jennie's expression softened, but the sadness in her eyes remained. "Yes, I had a much different picture of your future than parenthood at this age."

The silence returned, heavy with unspoken fears and shattered expectations. Kyla felt the weight of the moment, wondering how she could reconcile her truth with the daughter her mother thought she knew.

Finally, Jennie broke the silence, her voice tentative. "Who is the father?"

Kyla bit her lower lip, dreading this part. "His name is Jude," she said, her throat tightening. "No one you know, Mom. He worked at EarthSong for a little while, back in October, in exchange for food and lodging."

Kyla saw Jennie's eyes narrow slightly as she processed the information. "I see. And does he know you're pregnant?"

"No. And I don't know where he is. I don't even know his last name. EarthSong doesn't keep records of its workers. That'd be a full-time job," Kyla explained, her voice wavering.

"If you could contact him, would you?"

Kyla hesitated, her mind racing. The thought of reaching out to Jude felt impossible, like trying to catch smoke.

Jennie stood and moved closer, placing her hands on Kyla's shoulders. "Listen, honey, accidents happen. Even with the best of intentions, even with married couples. That's just life."

Tears welled up in Kyla's eyes as her mother's words sank in.

"Don't beat yourself up about this, not even for a second. Your family is here for you. Always." Jennie's hands loosened on her shoulders, her touch a small comfort amid Kyla's swirling emotions.

"Thanks, Mom," Kyla whispered, her voice thick with gratitude. "You're the best. Your support means everything."

Jennie gave her a gentle smile. "Now, how about this? I'll pick you up at the commune tonight around 7:00. Do you think you'll be ready by then?"

Kyla thought for a moment, the rush of packing was daunting but manageable. She nodded. "Yeah, I'll be ready."

Jennie added, "Clay and I will come help you move your things. He can secure your bike in the truck's rack."

Kyla let out a soft laugh, the sound bright after the intensity of the morning. With her mother's support and a plan in place, she felt a quiet hope—a ray of sunlight cutting through the lingering clouds of uncertainty.

Chapter Twenty-Seven

Jennie watched as Clay placed the last of Kyla's belongings in the barn. She overheard him say to Kyla, "You know, it feels good to see your things back here at the homestead."

Clay's tall frame stood out against the backdrop of hay bales and weathered timber, the fading evening light casting him in a golden glow. To Jennie, he looked like he'd stepped straight out of a country music video—rugged, handsome, and unmistakably cowboy.

Drawn to him, she stepped closer, slipped an arm around his waist, and gave him a quick squeeze.

Clay responded with a warm kiss on her cheek. "Never a dull moment around here, darlin'," he said with a smile.

Jennie smiled, soaking in the comfort of Clay's presence. Her gaze shifted to Kyla, who stood by the barn door, her face a blend of fatigue and relief.

"Oh, don't you worry, honey," Jennie said quickly, flashing Kyla a reassuring wink. "She can take care of herself."

Kyla returned the smile and stepped out into the chilly December evening, wrapping her arms around herself. "Thanks for the suggestion, Mom," she called over her shoulder. "Great idea for me to stay in the main house tonight. I'll tackle the cleanup in... I don't know... should I call it 'Unit Two'?"

Jennie chuckled, a soft laugh touched with nostalgia. "No, definitely not Unit Two, dear."

"Good," Kyla replied. "Sounds way too clinical. I get enough of that at work."

She paused, then added, "Maybe I'll come up with a name —if I decide to name it at all. Not sure if I want to hang a shingle or just... be, you know?"

Jennie nodded, her voice gentle. "I know exactly what you mean, sweetheart. Just being can be a very good thing now and then."

"The house shouldn't need much cleaning," Jennie mused, her voice carrying a blend of pride and wistful reflection. "It was sparkling after the last guests left—but that was two years ago."

She remembered that day vividly—the final morning of running her beloved B&B. It had felt like closing a well-worn book, filled with both triumph and heartbreak. There was pride in having built something from scratch, something people loved. But the forced closure during Covid had hit like a gut punch. Still, from those ashes had come an unexpected freedom—a chance to rediscover who she was beyond running a business.

She'd returned to yoga classes with Bev, dabbled in water-colours, and even tried—unsuccessfully—to coax Clay into playing tennis. And slowly, something in her had shifted. Friends began to say she looked more like her old self—the woman she'd been when Derrick was alive. Her step had a new lightness, her laughter bubbled up more freely, and her smile shone as brightly as ever.

Bev, never one to keep quiet, often told anyone who'd listen, "It's like she's finally let go of all that heaviness."

* * *

Jennie shared the news of Kyla's pregnancy with Clay while they waited in the car, giving Kyla space to gather her things at EarthSong.

He seemed momentarily stunned when she told him, his gaze fixed on the dashboard as he absorbed the news. But, as Jennie expected, his response came quickly and calmly.

"Then I'm even happier Kyla's coming back home," he said, placing a steady hand on her knee.

Jennie exhaled, the comfort of his touch grounding her.

"How's Mama feeling about all this?" he asked gently.

She took a moment, gathering her swirling thoughts. "Honestly, sweetheart, it's going to take some time for me to fully process the change. But I take comfort in knowing Kyla's heading in the right direction—at least for now."

"For now?" Clay repeated, a slight crease forming between his brows. "Do you think something might go wrong?"

Jennie shook her head. "No, not exactly. It's just... the father. Who knows if he'll show up again down the road?"

Clay gave her knee a reassuring squeeze. "We'll deal with whatever comes, together. Don't let the unknown steal your peace."

A warmth spread through Jennie at his words. There had been a time when she'd unfairly measured Clay against Derrick, caught between memory and moving on. But over the years, Clay had shown her that he was his own man—steadfast, kind, and quietly strong. She had come to love him deeply, and somehow, he had slipped into the fabric of their family as if he'd always belonged.

Chapter Twenty-Eight

Since Kathleen was already in bed by the time Jennie, Clay, and Kyla arrived home Friday night, Kyla felt a wave of relief—at least she wouldn't have to explain her sudden return to her grandmother right away.

"Don't worry," Jennie said gently, sensing her daughter's unease. "I'll talk to Mom when the time feels right."

"Okay, Mom, whatever you think," Kyla replied. "I just don't want to upset Grandma... but maybe it's better coming from you. Just promise you'll let me know once you've talked to her."

Jennie nodded.

Kyla was no longer anxious about speaking with Alexa. The concern Alexa had shown after her bicycle accident had sparked a glimmer of hope—maybe their once-strong bond could be rebuilt. Now, as she settled back into life at the homestead, Kyla felt steadier, more grounded than she had in months. The tea bread incident still lingered at the edges of her memory, but she was ready to move past it—and she hoped Alexa was, too.

* * *

The tires of Jennie's white Audi crunched over the gravel as she pulled into the parking lot of the indoor market on Saturday morning. As she stepped out of the car, her gaze landed on a trio of young women gathered near a hydro pole, their attention fixed on a cluster of brightly coloured music festival posters. They were around Alexa and Kyla's age, their laughter and lively chatter blending with the crisp morning air.

Moments later, Jennie heard the familiar rumble of Bev's car pulling in beside her. She glanced over just as Bev stepped out, her fiery red hair catching the morning light. Bev's wide smile was as bright as the sun itself.

"Good morning, Jen!" Bev's sing-song voice rang out as she approached. Jennie smiled warmly as Bev fell into step beside her, her pace quick and eager.

"You look particularly serene today," Bev remarked, her eyes twinkling with curiosity—an expression Jennie knew well. "A far cry from how you looked yesterday when you came back after lunch."

Jennie's smile tightened slightly. Bev, as always, didn't miss a beat when it came to commenting on people's moods or appearances.

Jennie raised an eyebrow, unsure if that was meant as a compliment. "Is that so?" she asked, keeping her tone light.

"Oh, yes. I'm beyond happy to announce that Kyla moved back to Cliffhouse last night," Jennie replied, her smile widening. Her joy was evident in the sparkle of her eyes. But as she spoke, she noticed the trio of young women shifting their focus from the posters to her. A sudden awareness of being watched made her lower her voice.

"Really?" Bev's eyebrows shot up, her surprise clear. "I'm

glad to hear you're happy. I know you and Alexa weren't exactly thrilled with EarthSong."

Jennie nodded, keeping her tone light and casual. Bev's curiosity had a way of spiraling into a full-on interrogation, and she wasn't in the mood for that today.

"And was there a particular reason Kyla moved out of EarthSong, Jen?" Bev's voice took on its familiar probing edge.

Jennie shrugged, waving a hand dismissively, her expression neutral. "Oh, you know, she'd been there for four years and just wanted a change of pace. That's all."

A sudden burst of laughter from the group of young women made Jennie's steps falter. One of them snickered louder than seemed natural, and Jennie couldn't shake the feeling it was aimed at her. She paused on the stairs, and Bev, ever perceptive, followed suit. The young women exchanged glances, a smirk tugging at one of their lips.

"Oh, brother," the woman muttered to her friends, her tone thick with sarcasm.

Jennie noticed Bev lift her chin slightly, as if catching a scent on the wind.

"Is Kyla still working at the vet clinic?" she asked, as though her curiosity hadn't quite been satisfied.

"No," Jennie said, a hint of regret in her voice. "I think she found the stress of working with Dr. Nicholls and his unpredictable moods a bit much... even though she said he'd lightened up a bit lately—smiles more now, she said."

"Hmm," Bev murmured. "Kyla loved working with animals. I wonder if there's more to the story—especially considering Dr. Nicholls' change in demeanor."

Jennie caught the mischievous glint in Bev's eyes just before her teasing grin spread wider.

"Ooh, maybe a new relationship is on the horizon," Bev said, her voice light with amusement.

Jennie chuckled as she watched Bev rub her hands together like a cat plotting its next move. The warmth of a blush crept up her cheeks, but she quickly tried to mask it with a playful tone.

"Oh, stop it, Bev," she said, swatting her friend's arm lightly. "Let's not jump to conclusions, dear friend." Her voice grew more serious as she added, "Relationships are complicated; I don't need to remind."

"Mm-hmm," Bev hummed, her knowing smile making it clear she thought she'd uncovered a juicy secret. "Still, I can see why it makes sense for Kyla to move back to Cliffhouse. Although you'd think she'd want her independence like Alexa. Maybe rent an apartment in Grace Square."

Jennie inwardly sighed as they climbed the stairs. Bev never left a stone unturned, always digging until she hit bedrock.

"We're just glad she's back," Jennie said, trying to steer the conversation away from a topic she wasn't ready to address. But even as she spoke, the laughter and whispers from the women behind them hung in the air, a reminder that no matter how carefully one treads, the truth has a way of slipping through the cracks.

"Ah, yes, that's perfect," Bev agreed, sensing that Jennie was done discussing it, at least for now.

Jennie inserted the hall key into the lock, but just as she did, another loud comment from the group by the post made her pause. "Ditched her friends and left without a word," said the one in the long peasant-style dress, her friends nodding and rolling their eyes in exaggerated agreement.

"Another bitch set to go after the swoony vet," one of them snipped.

Jennie turned the key in the lock, opened the door, and stepped inside with Bev following. As Jennie flicked on the lights, Bev closed the door behind them, her expression now darkened with curiosity.

"What was that about?" Bev asked, frowning.

"Town gossip, I guess," Jennie replied, trying to sound casual. "Sounds like some aren't happy with Kyla's sudden departure. As for the other remark... who knows what that's about?"

But deep down, Jennie couldn't shake the unease those whispers stirred. She hoped they were just idle chatter, but the sting lingered.

Chapter Twenty-Nine

Kyla slept soundly on Friday night. The sounds of Jennie leaving for the indoor market and Kathleen clattering dishes in the kitchen didn't disturb her rest.

Rising from her warm bed, Kyla padded across the cool floor in her bare feet, slid open a window on the east side of the house, and poked her head into the morning air. She inhaled deeply. A mix of scents that felt like home added to her contentment on Saturday morning. The fresh ocean breeze, musty hay, and the sweet aroma of evergreens conspired to make Kyla smile. A beam of morning sun traced a path across the front garden, where a few pink roses drooped their tired heads—the last of the outdoor summer flowers.

Glancing across to the greenhouse, Kyla pictured the welcoming blooms of cyclamens, Christmas cacti, kalanchoe, and poinsettias. Each year, they displayed a colourful array of red, white, and yellow blossoms, filling the gap between the winter and spring gardens. It was standard practice in the family for Kathleen's famous amaryllis to occupy their special place in the greenhouse, waiting to make their debut among the Christmas decorations in two weeks.

Washing her face with warm water, Kyla thought about when she might share the news with Alexa. Deciding that today would be a good day, since Alexa was off work and Kyla was feeling happy, she called her twin on her cellphone.

"Lexi, guess what?" she asked excitedly.

"I know," replied Alexa. "You've moved back home."

"How did you know? I didn't tell anyone." Kyla was puzzled. What could have changed? Was it Mom? Clay? Had her family been so excited that they couldn't wait to tell the world before she even got out of bed this morning?

"There are no secrets; you know that, Kye." Alexa chuckled, seizing the chance to tease her twin. She waited a few seconds before revealing her source.

"It was Graham," Alexa said, much to Kyla's surprise. "And I must admit I was more than a little miffed that he knew before I did," she huffed.

"Graham?" Kyla repeated. "I didn't think you were still seeing him. And how on earth did he know I'd moved back home?"

"Ah, you know the grapevine is alive and well on Sunrise Island, Kye," Alexa continued to tease.

"Okay," said Kyla, settling into an upholstered bedroom chair from yesteryear that still felt comfortable if you weren't too picky. "I'll ask the obvious. How did Graham find out?"

"He ran into Mom at The Sunrise Café and asked about us both."

"Oh, I see," said Kyla, happy to have the mystery solved. "So, you haven't reconnected with Graham yourself, then?"

"Ah, I don't know, Kye. We were never that connected in the first place," she said. "At least from my point of view."

"That's what I thought, Lex. But you never know. Relationships are tricky, that's for sure."

"So, listen," said Alexa, "why don't I stop by this afternoon and help you move in?"

"Ha," laughed Kyla. "I was calling to see if you could drop by today, but not to help me move in. I have something exciting to tell you." Kyla surprised herself by using the word *exciting*. That wouldn't have been her choice of words only yesterday.

Chapter Thirty

Kyla bounced downstairs, still in her bare feet, and waltzed into the sunny kitchen. "Grandma, do you know how happy I am to see you this morning?" she asked, reaching out to embrace Kathleen.

Kathleen's startled expression reminded Kyla that her grandmother had gone to bed before she arrived last night and likely wouldn't have known she'd stayed over unless Jennie told her this morning.

With one hand on her chest, Kathleen stepped back, eyes wide. "Kyla, I had no idea you were here," she exclaimed.

"Grandma, I'm so sorry. I thought Mom would have told you this morning," Kyla said, her voice softening with guilt.

"No, no. I didn't see her before she left for the market." Kathleen smiled warmly. "But, what a lovely surprise, dear. Are you staying for the weekend?"

Kyla hadn't anticipated this reaction. She moved toward the coffee pot, trying to buy herself a moment to think. As she opened the cupboard and removed a coffee mug, she poured herself a full cup, replying slowly, "Yes, yes, Grandma. And I have some good news."

"Oh, I'm all ears, Kyla," Kathleen said, pulling out a chair to sit at the small kitchen table. "Please, have a seat," she added, stirring a teaspoon of sugar into her coffee.

Kyla's mind raced as she approached the table. *I can tell Grandma I'm moving in, but Mom promised to break the bigger news. But I plan to tell Alexa about the baby today... How can I tell Alexa and not Grandma? And she'll want to know why I moved back.*

Kyla sat down and tested a sip of hot coffee, smiling over the rim at her grandmother. The coffee mug in her hands was one her mother had crafted for use in the B&B.

Setting the cup down, Kyla reached out and held Kathleen's hands in hers. "Grandma," she said tenderly, "I'm going to live here now, in the side-by-side."

"Kyla, that's a dream come true for me," Kathleen replied, her voice filled with emotion. "Cliffhouse is big enough for all of us. I want the whole family to live here, where they belong. But this is a good start. Now we'll just have to work on your sister."

"Yes," Kyla smiled, feeling a warmth spread through her. "And," she ventured, "there's something else."

"Uh oh," Kathleen muttered, her tone shifting, "I feel like maybe some not-so-good news is coming my way."

"Well," Kyla replied, choosing her words carefully, "it depends on how you look at it."

"What is it, dear?" Kathleen asked, leaning forward on the table, her eyes locked on Kyla's.

"I'm going to have a baby, Grandma."

Silence filled the sunny kitchen, interrupted only by the hum of the fridge. Kathleen sat still, saying nothing. Kyla watched in horror as her grandmother's face turned pale, and before she could react, Kathleen tumbled onto the floor, her eyes shut.

Horrified, Kyla dropped to her knees beside Kathleen, her breath catching in her throat. "Grandma, no!" she cried, her voice trembling as she pressed two fingers to Kathleen's neck. The pulse was faint, barely there, but it was something. Leaning in close, she could feel the soft, shallow breaths against her cheek.

Panic surged through Kyla. Racing to the wall phone, she fumbled with the receiver, her fingers shaking as she dialed 911. "Please, hurry," she managed to choke out to the operator before hanging up.

She threw open the kitchen door, her heart pounding. "Clay!" she screamed into the empty morning air, the word echoing off the trees. *He's probably paragliding*, she realized with a sinking feeling. Desperate, she dialed his cellphone, leaving a message that barely made sense in her panic.

Returning to the kitchen, she grabbed a pillow and blanket from the living room but hesitated when she saw Kathleen's still form on the floor. *What if it's a stroke? I won't move her.* She tucked the wool blanket around Kathleen's legs instead, her mind racing with every bit of first-aid training she could remember.

The suffocating silence offered no comfort, only deepening her concern with every passing second. When Rollo's bark finally reached her ears, it was like a lifeline. She ran to the door, relief flooding her as she yelled out to the paramedics what had happened.

"She's eighty-four now," Kyla muttered, guilt tightening her chest. *This is my fault. I should have waited for Mom to tell her. What else can I mess up?* The thought clawed at her as she pulled on her jacket and climbed into the ambulance beside Kathleen. Tears blurred her vision as she stroked her grandmother's arm, the familiar warmth now terrifyingly fragile.

"Please, Grandma," she whispered, as the ambulance doors slammed shut. The paramedic directed Kyla to sit back and secure her seatbelt. The siren wailed to life, amplifying the fear in Kyla's heart.

* * *

Jennie rushed out of the bustling market as soon as she received Kyla's call. She didn't bother scolding Kyla for ignoring her advice on the best time to tell Kathleen bad news. Still, she couldn't shake the sinking feeling of disappointment in Kyla's judgement.

Of greater importance as Jennie headed her Audi toward Lady Minto Hospital was how her mother was doing.

* * *

"Her shoulder seemed to take the brunt of the fall," Jennie explained to Dr. Bell, the attending physician.

Kathleen had regained consciousness but still appeared pale. She offered Kyla a faint smile as her granddaughter held her hand, while she lay in bed with her legs elevated.

"Does your mother experience dizziness?" Dr. Bell inquired.

"Yes," Jennie replied quickly, recalling her mother's fall from a kitchen stool three years ago. "She has low blood pressure," she added, "and decreased vision in her left eye, likely due to a cataract, according to her optometrist."

"I see," Dr. Bell acknowledged. "The X-rays don't show any fractures, fortunately, but there is a healed fracture in her right wrist."

"Yes," Jennie confirmed, "from the fall three years ago."

Turning toward Kathleen, Dr. Bell raised his voice to help her hear. "Do you feel ready to go home, Kathleen? Or would you prefer to rest here for a day or so?"

Without hesitation, Kathleen weakly responded, "Home to Cliffhouse," before closing her eyes, as if imagining the cheerful blooms in her greenhouse rather than the concerned faces of the adults gathered around her.

* * *

By the time Alexa arrived at the hospital, the immediate crisis had passed. She had called Kyla on her way, her voice tight with concern.

"What happened? How did Grandma fall off the kitchen chair?"

Kyla's voice trembled as she explained, "Shock. She was shocked by the news that I'm pregnant."

Alexa fell silent, stunned.

"I'm so sorry, Lexi," Kyla continued, her words rushing out. "I didn't want you to find out this way. And it's all my fault that Grandma lost her balance and fell after hearing the news."

"Uh, okay," Alexa replied, her voice strained. "I'll be at the hospital in about five minutes. We can talk later."

* * *

As the family gathered on the verandah at Cliffhouse, the sun dipping low in the sky, Kathleen offered her blessings to Kyla. "Kyla, dear, don't you worry about a thing," she said, her voice light and reassuring. "I've been around the block so many times, there's very little that qualifies as news anymore," she laughed softly, easing the tension in the air.

The warm comfort of the verandah embraced them all, a peaceful Sunday afternoon scene. Kathleen, wrapped in her favourite fuchsia-coloured angora blanket, settled near the outdoor heater. She took a sip of her home-grown jasmine tea, and the colour had returned to her cheeks, her energy restored.

"And you know," she added, her voice a little lighter, "I won't lie. I can't wait to hear the patter of little feet at Cliff-house again." Her smile spread warmly across her face, filling the space with the familiar, soothing affection only she could offer. "I'll start working on a crocheted pink baby blanket tomorrow," she said to Kyla, her eyes twinkling.

Earlier that week, during her lunch break, Kyla had browsed through a second-hand baby clothing rack, daydreaming about whether the baby would be a boy or a girl. "Girls do seem to predominate in the Mitchell family," Kathleen added with a wink, keeping her tone light and playful.

Kyla grinned, joining in the banter. "You're going to follow up that pink blanket with a blue toque, aren't you, Grandma?"

Kathleen chuckled, her eyes sparkling with mischief. "I like to roll the dice," she said with a shrug. "Besides," she added with a grin, "I can whip up a whole new wardrobe in blue, if necessary, in the drop of a hat... pardon the pun, sweetheart."

Chapter Thirty-One

"Would you mind if I brought Emily home for Christmas, Mom?" asked Nick on one of his infrequent calls to Jennie.

Jennie had just stepped out of a long-awaited relaxation bath just after supper on Sunday evening. Conversation at the supper table had been cordial and non-dramatic. It seemed to Jennie as if everyone was ready for some quiet time.

Jennie listened as Alexa's voice drifted up from the floor below, the evening winding down into quiet. "Good night, Grandma," Alexa said, her tone gentle as she bent to kiss Kathleen on the cheek.

"Lexi, I'm sure we'll catch each other on the ride home from work," Kyla said, giving her sister a quick hug. Jennie watched from her bedroom window as Alexa stepped off the verandah and headed toward her car. Rollo eagerly trotted after her, his tail wagging in the soft night air.

Jennie wrapped an enormous bath towel around herself and plopped down in one of her bedroom chairs to talk with Nick on her cellphone.

"Emily? Isn't she going home for her own family Christmas, dear?"

"Normally she would, Mom, but she said it's too expensive for her to fly back to England so close to graduation."

"Yes, I see what you mean. And you graduate in June next year, isn't that right, dear?"

"Provided I pass all the board exams, Mom. That's an unknown. The Canadian boards are known to be tough."

"What an accomplishment it will be, then, when you sail through with flying colours," Jennie encouraged.

"So, what about Christmas, Mom?"

"Uh, I need a moment to think, Nick. Let me see... Kyla will be in one half of the side-by-side...Oh," exclaimed Jennie, suddenly realizing that Nick wouldn't be caught up on family news. And then her heart sank. *Oh boy, I'm just not going there again tonight.*

"What? What is it, Mom?" asked Nick, having heard Jennie's exclamation.

"Oh, ha," Jennie fibbed, "I almost spilled tea on my lap. Now," she continued, "we'll have Kyla, Alexa, Clay, Kathleen, you, and me. That's five in a four-bedroom house. That's one reason Kyla will be staying in the side-by-side."

Thinking she smoothed that one over pretty well, Jennie moved on to the topic of Patrick. "By the way, dear, do you remember meeting Clay's son Patrick a few years back? He'd visited his dad when Clay lived at the old Johnson farm on the island."

Nick was silent for a moment. "Ah, yes, I have a vague recollection of a tall, slim dude who looked a lot like Clay," Nick replied.

"He does," said Jennie. "It looks like he may also be joining us over the holidays."

"I see. So, is that your way of telling me there wouldn't be room for my true love?" he asked, playfully.

"Ah, so Emily is your true love, now, is she? This is the first I've heard of such a thing," Jennie said, playing along.

"I guess it's neither here nor there in the end, Mom," responded Nick. "Come June, she'll be gone, so that's the end of that tune," he said, sounding a little deflated, Jennie thought.

"Okay, Nick. I'm looking forward to hearing all about Emily over the holidays. And, yes, of course, she's welcome to celebrate Christmas with us. She'll have to stay in your room, dear; is that okay?" Jenny asked, tongue in cheek.

"Um, Mom, I think that would be such a novelty," Nick replied, laughing good-heartedly.

And then, Jenny couldn't help herself. "Accidents do happen, my love, so please take care."

"Mom, I'm not sixteen anymore," replied Nick. "But we'll take that under advisement," he added, chuckling out loud. Jennie didn't miss Nick's tone, a mixture of annoyance and amusement.

I had to say it, corny or not, Jenny told herself. "Okay, dear, maybe you two can pop into the Christmas market on December 17. It'd mean the world to me."

"That'll work, Mom. If it's anywhere near as perfect as three years ago, I'm sure my lady love will go wild."

Nick didn't know about Kyla's pregnancy yet, and Jennie didn't want to add any more stress on top of his mid-term studies. They'd just have to wait until he was home in two weeks.

Chapter Thirty-Two

Kyla was grateful that Clay offered to help her find a vehicle. The distance to the vet clinic was too far for her to bike, especially in bad weather. Plus, Clay and Jennie were far too busy with their own schedules to keep driving Kyla to and from work.

On Monday, he picked her up after her shift, loading her bicycle into the back of his black paragliding van.

"You'll need a reliable vehicle," Clay said. "Something safe for both you and the baby, with enough room for a car seat, stroller, diaper bag, blankets... I can hardly remember all the stuff we used to haul around when Patrick was a baby."

Kyla mused. *This man knows something about raising kids.*

With few expenditures beyond recycled clothing and basic necessities, Kyla had saved a good deal over the years. Vacations, like the meditation retreat on Cortez Island, were rare. She and her friends often went on weekend kayak trips, sleeping in tents and cooking over an open fire. She liked her simple lifestyle. As for the future, she could only imagine.

Though Kyla had thought about buying an electric vehicle,

Clay cautioned her. "There've been too many recall alerts lately. Have you seen those videos showing fires breaking out? That'll make you think twice."

Since her father, Derrick, had passed away four years ago, the twins had come to appreciate Clay's fatherly influence. Nick hadn't been around much since their dad's death, so they hadn't bonded in the same way. But Clay had seamlessly integrated into the family—at least, that's how it seemed to Kyla.

Kyla ultimately decided on a silver 2024 Subaru Forester. The roomy backseat was a key factor, especially since she'd need to maneuver to fasten a car seat. Despite Clay's suggestion of a Volvo XC60, the idea of upgrading from an ecovillage lifestyle to driving a luxury car didn't sit well with her.

Clay helped Kyla negotiate a price she was comfortable with. Since it was her first car purchase, she had no idea what constituted a good deal. When they landed on the final cost, Clay's eyes widened in surprise, but before he could react, Kyla said, "That's fine. I'll write a cheque for the full amount."

That moment was seared into Kyla's memory. Losing her father, Derrick, so suddenly had been hard enough. But Jennie's added stress over an unexpected debt made it even worse. Derrick had secretly purchased a vacation to celebrate their anniversary, leaving Jennie with unexpected financial pressure. Watching her mother struggle with mounting debt, on top of other financial concerns, left a lasting impact on Kyla. There was no way she'd finance her vehicle.

* * *

Kyla beamed with pride as she drove her new car up the gravel drive at Cliffhouse. The fresh, new-car smell reminded her of Jennie's joy when she bought her Audi.

Shutting off the engine, Kyla glanced into the back seat,

imagining her baby tucked into a car seat. Even though she was only two months along, she looked forward to the swelling of her belly. Now that her morning sickness had subsided, she felt more content with her circumstances. With her family close by, Kyla was gaining confidence, reassured that things were becoming more manageable—and happier. She realized she hadn't given EarthSong another thought since leaving last Friday evening.

Kyla placed a hand on Clay's shoulder and stretched up to kiss his cheek. With a quick peck, she said gratefully, "Thank you so much, Clay. I had no idea what to buy, how much to pay, or how to bargain..."

She heard Clay's soft laugh as he pulled her into a warm hug. "You're going to be a great mama, Kyla—just like Jennie."

Kyla's heart warmed at his words. His confidence in her sparked a small degree of confidence in herself. She was starting to think of herself as a mother, but it still felt a little distant. She had no clear idea what being a mother would involve, but for now, her main concern was the pregnancy itself.

That reminded her... her next appointment with Dr. Shelley was this Wednesday. *I'm going to mention that weird thing with the charcoal,* she thought, suddenly recalling the strange incident over the weekend.

While sitting in front of a wood-burning fire, Kyla had felt nauseous and had to leave the room. For some reason, her mind kept fixating on the charcoal in the bottom of the fireplace grate. And even stranger, she imagined herself eating it.

Chapter Thirty-Three

After such an eventful Monday, Kyla felt happy but exhausted as she entered the main house through the kitchen door. Emerging from the dining area, Kathleen greeted her warmly.

"Hello, darling, supper will be ready in another half hour. Your mom should be home soon. She and Bev are putting in pretty long days at the market hall."

"I know," replied Kyla. "They're an amazing pair. Two peas in a pod."

"Yes," chuckled Kathleen. They were a bit distanced when Jennie was so tied up with the B&B, but that's all changed, and it's so much the better for your mom's health."

"Yeah, Mom looks great, doesn't she?"

"Sure does, dear, but I must say that you look a bit weary. Did you and Clay have any luck with your car shopping?"

"Grandma, come and see my new Forester," Kyla said excitedly with a resurgence of energy.

* * *

Jennie, Clay, Kyla, and Kathleen gathered around the table for supper after a weekend full of emotions—revelations, reconciliations, and a mix of happy and sad events that left them all feeling drained.

"I think I'll just do a light dusting in my new place," Kyla announced, "and then hit the hay early."

Kathleen, with a warm smile, looked up at Kyla and replied, "No need to dust, sweetheart. Your new home is already shining. I took care of it while you were at work, and now it's ready for the special touches only you can add."

Jennie gasped. "Oh, Mom, you are the sweetest. I hope you didn't overdo it."

Kathleen chuckled softly. "Don't worry, dear. I'm more careful these days. After a broken wrist and a second fall, I've learned to listen to my body."

Kyla slid back in her chair and walked around the table, placing a kiss of gratitude on her grandmother's cheek. "You couldn't have done anything more thoughtful, Grandma. I love you so much. I can't wait to cook dinner for you once I get settled in."

Kathleen laughed lightly. "And I can walk over there by myself. Now that's something I like."

Clay smiled and nodded at Kathleen. "I admire your independence and feisty spirit. It'll keep you strong for years to come."

"That's the plan," Kathleen replied, giving a small nod.

"I'll take care of the cleanup, Mom. Do you want to sit on the verandah tonight, or is it too chilly?" Clay asked.

"I turned the heaters on and moved one right by your favorite settee," he reassured her. "But it's entirely up to you, Kathleen. Jennie and I will probably head out there after we clean up."

Kyla entered her new home, her overnight bag in hand, and

was greeted by a neatly organized pile of her belongings on the floor. A window was slightly open, letting in a refreshing breeze from the sea, and the house smelled inviting. The space was calm, orderly, and clean—a stark contrast to the chaos of the weekend. The familiar warmth of her childhood memories settled over her as she took in the surroundings, just as she had felt in the main house. She felt a deep sense of belonging, comforted by the sight of her new SUV parked outside and the knowledge that she finally had a place to call her own.

After picking out clothes for work the next day, she prepared for bed. The soft mattress welcomed her, and she fell asleep almost instantly, content and at peace.

Chapter Thirty-Four

Kyla was surprised to receive a text from Dr. Nicholls only days after she'd left her job at the vet clinic. Hearing from him this way was unexpected—bumping into him around town would have felt more natural.

Her tone was more relaxed than it might've been when she worked for him, but those formalities no longer applied.

* * *

Kyla spotted Dr. Nicholls' champagne-coloured BMW convertible the moment she pulled into the parking lot. With the top down, it was hard to miss. As she parked, he stepped out of the car. He looked especially handsome this morning, she thought—his off-white shirt highlighted his dark features. The sporty look was a side of him she wasn't used to seeing.

They ordered tall drinks to go and left the café, strolling toward the harbour.

"Beautiful winter day, isn't it, Dr. Nicholls?" Kyla said, taking in the crisp sea air.

"Please—call me Harry," he said with a smile. "Yes, Dr. Nicholls at the clinic—if you ever decide to come back," he added lightly. "But outside of work, it's just Harry."

"It'll take some getting used to," Kyla admitted. Then she gave it a try. "Have you found another assistant yet, Harry?" The name felt unfamiliar on her tongue, but not unpleasant.

"A temp from an agency, for now," he replied with a slight shrug. "We'll see how it goes."

"I'm sure it'll take time to find the right fit, Harry," she said, gently emphasizing his name. She sipped her drink.

"The right one's walking beside me," he said, half-joking, before quickly adding, "But I'm not here to talk you into coming back."

They reached a small cove where a bench overlooked the water, perfectly placed to catch the morning light. They sat, coffees in hand.

"How's your pregnancy going, Kyla?" Harry asked. "You must be starting to show now, right?"

"Soon," she nodded. "There's a bump, but it's easy to hide under layers. I'm feeling great, though—and I love being back at Cliffhouse."

"I can imagine," he said. "That place has a legacy. I've heard stories about the Mitchell family for years."

"Have you never been to the farm?" Kyla asked, surprised.

"Nope," he admitted with a chuckle. "I've driven by and craned my neck trying to see through the trees, but that's it."

"Well, we'll have to change that. You do know the whole island's invited to our Open House on December 23rd, right? We skipped two years during the pandemic, but it used to be a big thing."

"I've heard of it, but back then, my ex and I would usually spend the holidays in Hawaii. We were always away that week."

"Then I'm inviting you this year," Kyla said, pleased by how natural their conversation had become. "I'll text you a reminder. It starts at four—just in time for the tree lighting and all the after-dark rituals. It's kind of a winter wonderland, even if we don't get actual winter."

Harry laughed. "I know what you mean. The first time I spent Christmas in Hawaii, it felt surreal. I'm from Ontario—Christmas lights on palm trees didn't quite do it for me."

Kyla nodded, understanding. "At least here we get a bit of snow sometimes. A white Christmas still feels magical."

"Not this year, though," Harry said, glancing around. "I'm not even wearing a coat. And my convertible top's down. That pretty much says it all."

A comfortable silence settled between them as they sat watching the sun's reflection shimmer across the harbour. Then, quietly, Harry broke it.

"I'm a little rusty at this," he said, his voice tentative. He glanced sideways before continuing. "I was wondering... would you like to go hiking with me this weekend?"

A sweet, slightly nervous smile curved his lips—one that made Kyla look at him a little longer than she intended.

"Oh," she said, caught off guard but smiling back. "I—uh—well, I'd love to go hiking, Harry. I could use the exercise, and it's always nicer with company."

Is he asking me out? she wondered. *This is quite a turn of events.* The man she once resented for his arrogance now seemed almost bashful, as vulnerable as a schoolboy.

But the invitation had come out of nowhere. She needed time to process it.

"Shall we keep walking?" she said, rising from the bench and brushing the edge of her coat. "Too much sitting isn't great when you're pregnant, or so I've been told."

They fell into step again, their pace unhurried, but Kyla's thoughts moved quickly.

Conflicting feelings stirred. She couldn't ignore how different Harry seemed outside the clinic—warm, open, even a little unsure of himself. But the memory of their past interactions lingered, like a splinter under the skin. There were too many times—far too many—when he'd been curt, dismissive, even harsh. Not in front of clients, of course, but behind closed doors, he could be difficult. She vividly remembered the day he'd snapped at her over a double-booked appointment, his words sharp enough to leave a bruise.

People change, she thought. *But do they? And if they do—how do you know when it's real?*

But Kyla wasn't fooling herself. She knew full well how attractive Harry was. *Tall, dark, and handsome* fit him to a tee. Still, looks only went so far. That kind of appeal faded quickly when not backed by something more substantial, and Kyla had learned to prioritize different qualities.

She valued intelligence, and Harry had plenty of that. His reputation among peers was solid—she'd overheard praise at veterinary conferences over the years. And she'd seen firsthand the respect he commanded at the clinic. Clients rarely second-guessed his advice, even in the most difficult situations. Some even thanked him after their beloved pets passed, a testament to the trust and grace he offered in moments of grief.

And really, she thought, *who doesn't love an animal lover?*

"How does Saturday morning sound?" Harry asked, breaking into her thoughts. "If the weather holds, we could hike up Mount Maxwell—if you're up for it."

Kyla hesitated, her gaze lingering on his face. She had to admit it—she'd always been attracted to him, despite the arrogance and occasional gruffness. *What would it even be like to date Dr. Harry Nicholls?* she mused. *Not that I'm dating material for long. And who knows if I'll even want to date once the baby's here.*

"I'm up for it," she said at last. "Mount Maxwell is one of my favourite hikes."

"It's a date," Harry said, his smile spreading. "I could pick you up at Cliffhouse, if you'd like. Or—"

"I'll meet you there," Kyla said quickly. "In the parking lot at ten. That work for you?"

"Perfect," he replied. "I'll bring food and drinks—we'll make it a winter picnic."

Driving back to Cliffhouse, Kyla found herself smiling. Normally, she'd be the one planning the picnic, making sure everything was just right. But it felt oddly empowering to let Harry take the lead. For once, she could lean back and enjoy the role of the guest—or the princess—something she secretly liked to play, at least now and then.

And for now, she thought, *that's more than enough.*

* * *

After work the next day, Kyla headed to her regular prenatal appointment with Dr. Shelley. She was on the monthly schedule for now, which would shift to biweekly visits at week twenty-eight, and then weekly after week thirty-six until her due date. She appreciated that Dr. Shelley offered evening appointments—it made things easier to manage after work. Though she no longer felt obligated to worry about leaving Harry in the lurch, she knew how quickly clinic work could pile up in her absence.

"*Pica* is the term used to describe cravings for non-food items," Dr. Shelley explained with a reassuring tone. "It's fairly common in pregnancy—and in children, too. We'll run a blood test to check for mineral deficiencies, iron in particular. But it could also be your body's way of managing nausea."

Kyla nodded, relieved she wasn't imagining things—or losing her mind. As Dr. Shelley prepared the needle, Kyla looked away, her stomach tightening. A bad experience years ago with an unsteady hand had left her squeamish about needles ever since.

Later, as she pulled into her driveway, Rollo came bounding toward her, tail wagging furiously. She crouched to greet him, offering pets and vigorous rubs while he leaned against her affectionately.

"Okay, okay, that's enough," she laughed, standing up and heading to the door. But Rollo was quicker, nudging past her legs in an attempt to get inside.

"No, Rollo, you can't come in," she said firmly, waving him away with one hand while balancing her bag with the other.

Spotting Clay walking in from the fields, she called out, "Clay! Can you get Rollo?"

Clay gave a sharp whistle, and Rollo turned mid-step, bolting off toward him, clearly distracted by the promise of another adventure.

Kyla smiled as she watched them go. German short-haired

pointers were notorious for their energy, and Rollo for his shedding. Now that she had her own place, she'd decided to draw the line: no dog hair inside. She wanted everything spotless, fresh, and ready for the arrival of her little one in July.

Chapter Thirty-Five

Kyla's joy was unmistakable as she pulled her silver Forester into a parking spot at the base of Mount Maxwell. She immediately noticed Harry's champagne-coloured BMW parked three spaces over. The trails were still popular in December, especially on clear days like this, even with patches of snow lingering near the summit.

She removed the transponder key and locked her door—something not everyone on the island bothered with, though that was beginning to change. As she grabbed her backpack and zipped up her winter jacket, she tugged on a pair of fleece-lined gloves and pulled a knitted hat over her ears to ward off the crisp, sunlit morning air.

Harry was already walking toward her, his backpack slung over one shoulder, leather gloves on, and that familiar bright smile warming his face.

"Good morning," he said. "Nice ride." He gave her Forester an approving glance.

Kyla grinned. "Thanks. She's not flashy, but she's reliable."

After she showed him a few of the SUV's features, Harry

gestured toward the trailhead. "Looks like we've got a good day for it. I thought we could take the Armand and Mountain Trail loop, if you're up for it. It's been dry lately, so mud shouldn't be an issue—especially if we stick to the grassy ridgelines."

"Yes, I love that route," Kyla said. "The views will be incredible in this light."

"Should take about two hours each way," he added. "That work for you?"

From zero to four hours, Kyla thought. *In six years, we've never spent time together outside the clinic—and honestly, I preferred it that way. Now here I am, committing to a full hike, lunch, and what could easily turn into a game-changing conversation.*

"Yes," she said evenly, slipping into a diplomatic tone. "I've got a free day, and I'm looking forward to reaching Baynes Peak. Maybe I'll even make a snowman."

Harry laughed. "Then we'd better get going. I packed a proper lunch—so you won't be making that snowman on an empty stomach."

Kyla gave a small smile as they began walking toward the trail. *Let's see where this goes,* she thought.

* * *

A few trail runners passed them now and then, pausing at scenic lookouts before continuing. Kyla and Harry stopped occasionally, too, taking water breaks and soaking in the sweeping views. The trail offered a mix of terrain: steep inclines, snow-dusted ridges, and sunlit stretches lined with Garry oak meadows and gurgling stream-fed gullies. Old-growth Douglas firs towered above them, and dense stands of pine and cedar offered shade even on the tougher climbs.

Though the path could be treacherous in wet weather—

slick with mud and moss—today it was dry and quiet, the winter sun filtering through bare branches. The air was crisp, the silence broken only by birdsong and the occasional rustle of wildlife in the underbrush.

"I've been up here before when everything was socked in with fog," Harry said as they reached the summit. He paused, looking out across the Gulf Islands and beyond to the faint blue outlines of Vancouver.

After a quiet moment, he turned toward Kyla. "I think this day was made for us."

Kyla hesitated, caught off guard. The words lingered between them, more personal than she expected. Coming from a former employer, it felt... loaded. Like that wink he'd given her a few weeks ago after she'd sorted out the vaccine mix-up with the cats.

She didn't respond. Instead, she looked out at the view, letting the moment pass. The silence might have felt awkward to Harry, but to Kyla, it offered clarity.

Harry stepped away from the edge, his expression unreadable. He shrugged off his backpack and set it down. Kyla wandered a few steps to the right, giving them both a bit of space.

He pulled out a folded Mexican blanket—striped in charcoal, green, and white—and spread it neatly over a flat rock near the cliff's edge. "Come, have a seat," he said, gesturing warmly.

The sun hung high in the cloudless sky as they settled in. It wasn't a date—not officially, but the scene had the makings of one.

Harry unpacked smoked salmon bites, a selection of crackers, cream cheese, capers, and a generous sprinkle of fresh dill. He added small containers of pineapple-tomatillo salsa and cilantro slaw, both, he told her, from his own recipes.

The man cooks. That's always a good thing, Kyla thought, smiling.

She didn't usually care for smoked salmon, but the way Harry had paired it—flavourful, well-balanced, and beautifully arranged—won her over. She reached for seconds without hesitation.

As they ate, the wind carried the scent of pine, and the sea shimmered in the distance. Kyla let herself relax—for now. Whatever this was becoming, she didn't have to define it today.

A rainbow of fresh fruit and a slice of rich chocolate torte brought the picnic to a perfect close. From his elegant basket, Harry revealed two wine glasses and a chilled bottle of Chardonnay, carefully packed in an insulated bag with ice pockets.

Kyla smiled as he poured. "Normally, I'd love a glass of Chardonnay, Harry, but these days, water is my drink of choice." She lifted her glass in a gentle toast.

Harry nodded without missing a beat and topped off her water glass before pouring a second glass of wine for himself. After they cleared the remains of their small feast, he settled back onto the blanket and looked at her more seriously.

"Now," he began, "do you mind if I ask you a few questions?"

"I don't mind at all, Harry," she replied, calm and open. "In fact, I welcome it." She preferred that he take the lead—safer that way. She could be too honest sometimes, and it wasn't always to her advantage.

Harry didn't hesitate. "First of all—how's your pregnancy going?"

Bam. She blinked, startled. *Who starts with that on a first date?*

Kyla took a sip of water—too quickly—and coughed as it went down the wrong way. She stood, turning away from the blanket to regain her composure, silently cursing his uncanny precision.

When she returned, Harry held out a piece of bread. "Here," he said gently, "this might help."

She accepted it gratefully and took a bite, the dry bread easing the tickle in her throat.

"I'm sorry to be so direct," he said, the corners of his mouth lifting. "But you know what I'm like."

Kyla let out a soft laugh. "Let's circle back to that in a bit," she said. "But right now, I have a question for *you*: You didn't seem surprised when I told you I'm expecting a baby... How did you know?"

Harry leaned back on his elbows, clearly pleased. "Well, I *am* medically trained," he said with mock gravity. "And I've watched both my sisters go through pregnancy twice each. I'd say I have a decent sense for the signs."

He grinned. "Plus, those emotional outbursts—however well you masked them—didn't escape me. And then there was the sudden dashing to the bathroom... especially after Laurie brought in that homemade raspberry pie."

Kyla chuckled. "You never miss a thing, do you?"

"Not where you're concerned."

She glanced at him before looking away again, then said, "I'm two months along. Baby's due in July."

There was no hesitation in her voice, no plea for understanding or approval—just a statement of fact.

"By resigning, I spared you from lost work hours during pregnancy and childbirth," she added, lifting her chin. "So you might say I did you a favour."

The words sounded clean, deliberate. Not an apology. A declaration.

But as the silence stretched, Kyla clenched her teeth—a tension coiled from six years of early mornings, emergency calls, and late-night surgeries. She missed it more than she dared admit. Still, she'd made her choice.

Harry rose and stretched. "I don't know about you, but my legs are cramped. Want to head over to the logs?"

Kyla nodded, brushing crumbs from her lap. The logs—remnants from an old homestead—were perfectly placed to take in the sweeping view toward Vancouver Island. Whoever once lived here had chosen their perch well.

They settled onto the smooth, sun-warmed wood, adjusting their coats against the mountain breeze. A few moments passed before Harry broke the silence again.

"And is there a father on the scene?" he asked, his tone deliberately casual.

"There's a father, obviously," Kyla said with a wry smile. "But on the scene? No."

She watched his face closely as she answered, curious what he'd reveal, if anything. There it was: a flicker of something in his eyes. Hope, maybe? *But why?* she wondered. *What would he even hope for?*

Kyla shifted on the log, crossing one leg over the other. "Now, it's my turn," she announced, her tone light but pointed.

Harry gave her a wary glance.

"With all due respect," she continued, her eyes narrowing playfully, "why were you—or should I say, why are you—so miserable at work? I mean, come on... six years of Mr. Grumpy Pants?" She paused, watching him carefully. "And don't pretend you don't know what I'm talking about."

Harry turned toward the distant horizon, a faint smile on his lips. He didn't deny it—at least not outright.

Kyla caught the expression and took it as a good sign. *No offense taken,* she thought, satisfied. *And honestly? I wouldn't care if he had been offended. He had it coming.*

I put up with six years of short answers, sharp looks, and silence. And now? I don't work for him anymore.

Harry took a slow sip of his wine, then turned toward her, his expression thoughtful.

"If you want to know something about my so-called trans-formation—from ogre to decent guy—well... here goes."

Kyla raised an eyebrow but said nothing, letting him speak.

"I sometimes see myself in you, Kyla," he said, "as strange as that may sound after all this time." He paused briefly. "The day you caught the vaccine mix-up... it took me straight back to my clinical days at vet school. I was in my fourth year, wrap-ping up a 13-week placement. On the second-to-last day, I misheard the vet's instructions and injected a cat with ten times the recommended dose of Meloxicam."

He drew in a slow breath.

"The cat nearly died. They caught it, flushed his system with fluids, and he pulled through. But the mistake still sits with me. It always will."

Kyla stayed quiet, absorbing the confession. It was hard to imagine the precise, hyper-competent Dr. Nicholls making such a serious error. And yet, he had.

"Wow," she said at last. "That's... heavy. I'm sorry you've carried that for so long." She gave him a knowing glance, then added with a wry smile, "But I think we lost a pet-owner that day. So, you still win."

Harry's smile was faint, but his eyes held steady. "Stuff happens, Kyla. We're all just human. What matters is what we do 80 percent of the time. That's why—no exaggeration—I'll do whatever it takes to keep you at the clinic should you agree to return."

Kyla narrowed her eyes slightly, the playfulness returning to her voice. "Hmm. That's odd, Harry. What makes you think I might leave?"

"I can't put my finger on it, Kyla," Harry said, playing along. "It's just that there've been a lot of changes in your life recently. You moved away from the ecovillage where you'd lived for four years, you're expecting a baby, and, as far as I know, planning to raise the child on your own. Those are sweeping changes. I just didn't want your employment with me to change along with the rest."

Kyla smiled gently, caught off guard by the quiet honesty from someone usually so guarded.

"You may have noticed that I love animals," she said. "And I'm pretty loyal when I'm comfortable in my surroundings and committed to my goals," her tone light but sincere.

"'Comfortable in your surroundings,' huh? Are you trying to tell me I was the problem?" Harry asked, half-smiling, half-cringing.

Kyla didn't miss the opening.

"Which brings me to my next question. Did something happen to you in your past to cause you to have a grumpy approach to life?" she asked with a slight furrow in her brow. "I know your patients adore you—your animal patients and their owners. But I see you act differently with them than you do with me."

"I won't deny the truth of what you said, Kyla," Harry admitted. "I've undergone some therapy to help me understand why I behave the way I have with you."

The word *therapy* stopped her cold. She hadn't imagined their strained dynamic had affected him that deeply. Kyla stayed silent, waiting for him to go on.

"I'll be honest with you, Kyla—since you've been honest with me. If you don't mind me airing a little dirty laundry," he said, glancing at her for permission.

"Go on, Harry," she replied, managing a light tone. "I'd actually like to know what makes you tick."

"You see, my ex, Debra, practically idolized me at first. I thought we were compatible and head-over-heels in love when we married, but things turned out differently when I made some bad investments and almost lost the house."

"Oh no, how stressful," Kyla said softly, though she couldn't quite imagine what it felt like to be married, to nearly lose everything.

"I treated Debra like a queen, and she took full advantage of that. But when I could no longer keep up with the lifestyle she'd grown used to, her affection cooled—subtly at first, then all at once."

"We'd talked about having a baby—it was something I pictured clearly. Coming from a big family, I'd always imagined I'd be a father someday. But for Debra, staying in shape and living comfortably seemed more important than starting a family."

Harry seemed to want to talk, so Kyla didn't interrupt. "She never liked animals. We owned a trio of Ridgebacks, beautiful dogs, but she didn't care for them. To make our lifestyle work, though, she kept up a facade when she thought it might further her personal goals. For example, she'd brush their coats until they shone, and then she'd spend hours in the boudoir pampering herself as she cleaned away any vestige of canine. But she didn't fool me."

He spoke with a kind of dry amusement, but Kyla could hear the weight beneath it—these weren't just old stories; they were the scaffolding of who he'd become.

As Harry took a sip of wine, Kyla asked,

"So... you and Debra eventually split?"

"She left me for a real estate hotshot in California," he said with a shrug. "Apparently, he made a fortune selling mansions to celebrities. I heard through the grapevine they're not together anymore."

Kyla tilted her head. "And why tell me all this, Harry?"

His directness seemed to be rubbing off on her.

Harry met her eyes. "Because I want you to know I appreciate your loyalty. Despite my, let's say... less-than-sunny disposition, you've stuck with me for six years. That means more than I've ever said out loud."

Not in her wildest dreams did Kyla ever think she'd be having this conversation with Dr. Nicholls. The man sitting beside her on the log felt like a stranger, far more likable than the one she'd known less than a week ago.

"Thank you for sharing all that, Harry," Kyla said, her voice soft. "And now, I have another question for you." She swallowed hard, uncertain where this conversation might lead.

"By inviting me here today, with this incredible picnic and sharing such personal details of your life... well..."

Harry cut her off, sparing her the awkwardness of voicing the obvious. He rose to his feet and extended a hand to help her up. Keeping hold of her hand, he led her to a breathtaking view, where a BC ferry made its steady way through the narrow passage below.

"I think you and I would make a good team outside of work, just as we do at work," he stated emphatically.

Harry turned to face her, his hand gently brushing under her chin, guiding her lips toward his.

Kyla closed her eyes, giving in to the moment, immersing herself in his expression of affection. When they parted, Harry asked, "How do you feel about that, Kyla?"

It took her a moment to find her footing, as though the ground beneath her had shifted.

"Harry, I don't understand," Kyla said softly, her voice laced with genuine confusion. "With your looks, your intelligence, your skills... Why would you even consider dating someone who's expecting?"

"I knew that would cause your head to spin," he said with a chuckle.

"But I'm not like everyone else. After being with a woman who was only after my money, I had to rethink my approach to relationships. It's been seven years since she left, and I've taken my time getting back into the dating scene." He smiled, a slight edge of vulnerability in his expression. "I've dated, sure, but none of them have made me feel the way you do."

"You have a funny way of showing it," Kyla couldn't help but tease. "Kind of like the schoolboy who makes life miserable for the girl he secretly likes."

"I guess that's one way to look at it," Harry said with a smile. "But my question still stands." He winked at her.

Kyla looked at Harry with new eyes. He'd shown her his vulnerability and warmth, letting her know just how much he appreciated her. The fact that she was pregnant didn't seem to faze him. Maybe a baby would satisfy his own longing for parenthood, should they become a committed couple.

"All I can say right now, in all honesty, Harry," she began slowly, "is that I'd like to give it a try. I'll keep an open mind. But we need to talk about what happens if it doesn't work out."

Their lips met again in a warm, lingering kiss before Harry pulled away, a playful glint in his eyes. "If it were only up to me, Kyla, I can tell you right now that it will work out. You're the wildcard, my dear."

He laughed, gathering the last of the picnic things. "Our future is all up to you."

Kyla took a deep breath, her mind still a whirl of emotions. She'd made up her mind. Her heart had won out over her doubts.

"Alright, Harry," she said, meeting his eyes. "I'll be back on Monday. I'm willing to give this a try."

Chapter Thirty-Six

Alexa stretched, arms reaching overhead, still wrapped in the warmth of her bed on a rare, slow Saturday morning. Sleeping in until ten wasn't typical for her, but after last night's run, she'd finally gotten the deep rest she'd been craving. It hadn't been an easy road since early November.

In just half an hour, she was meeting Graham for coffee at The Treehouse Café. Kyla had texted earlier—she'd be out hiking with her employer, which caught Alexa a little off guard. *It's sunny, so they'll enjoy themselves no matter what,* she thought.

Although Alexa knew her mom and Bev were just a short walk away at the market hall, she decided against dropping by. *Sometimes you need space, even from the ones you love,* she reasoned. *And today is one of those days.*

When Alexa arrived at The Treehouse, Graham had already claimed a table beneath one of the outdoor heaters.

"I thought you'd beat me here," she said with a smile, slipping into the chair across from him. "You're my most reliable friend." Then, more to herself, she added under her breath, "And predictable."

She had deliberately thrown on her dull gray sweatsuit, not wanting to send mixed signals—especially with the conversation she knew lay ahead. She adored Graham, but it was time to clarify where they stood.

"I ordered us two lattes," Graham said. "Figured the line would be long."

"Thanks," Alexa replied. "Good call."

"You look great this morning, Lex," he said, his eyes lighting up. "Vibrant, even."

Not the look I was going for, Alexa thought.

"That's nice of you, Graham. How was your night?"

His grin widened. "Better than I imagined," he said, clearly pleased.

"How so?" Alexa asked, genuinely glad he'd had a good time.

"I met someone," Graham said, eyes lighting up like embers as he launched into a story about meeting a newcomer named Savannah at the community dance hall.

Alexa froze, caught off guard. When he finished and the lattes arrived, all she could manage was, "I'm happy for you, Graham." She offered a brief smile, raising her cup and blowing gently on the steam.

"Really, Lex? Are you happy for me?"

The look in his eyes made her pause. *Why would he ask me that?*

"Does it matter what I think, Graham?" she replied carefully. "What matters is that you're happy."

"You know, Lex," he said, leaning in a little, "I had a great time with Savannah... but I kept wondering if you'd be jealous."

Regaining her composure, Alexa met his gaze. "To be honest, Graham, I thought you had feelings for me, more than just friendship. I came here today to let you know I don't feel the same way."

Graham looked down, his silence heavy.

"What's wrong, Graham?" she asked gently, placing her hand over his on the table.

Just then, Kevin Hunter passed by, glancing over and catching the moment between them. "Morning, Alexa," he said quickly. "Can't stop—catching a ferry. Have a good day."

As Kevin walked off, Alexa shifted uneasily. *What if he thinks I'm with Graham?* But at least Kevin had been alone.

Turning back to Graham, she continued, "Is something wrong?"

"No," he said after a pause, voice quiet. "I guess I always suspected you didn't feel the same... but I had to know for sure." He looked up at her. "The truth is, I do have strong feelings for you. But yeah... I suppose this is the part where we agree to just be friends."

Alexa gave him a tender look. "I've always valued our friendship, Graham. I'd be heartbroken to lose it."

He nodded, his expression unreadable. She thought she caught the shimmer of a tear in his eye.

"Me too, Lex," he said softly. "Thanks for being honest. I haven't been."

Alexa waited, sensing there was more.

"There's no Savannah," he admitted. "No sparks. I just... wanted to see if you'd react. The only sparks I've ever felt were with you."

"I'm sorry, Graham," Alexa said, her voice full of compassion. "Will you be okay?"

"More than okay," he said, straightening a little. "Knowing

the truth helps. Now I can move on. Let me cover the coffees, and I'll go find the *real* Savannah," he added with a small smile.

"Let's catch up in the new year, if I don't see you before then."

As she finished her coffee, Alexa smiled quietly to herself. She'd done the hard thing—honestly, kindly. And now, it was time to find her own sparks.

Chapter Thirty-Seven

Kyla woke up smiling on Sunday, December 11. Safe and cozy in her own home, she replayed yesterday's hike with Harry in her mind. It still surprised her that any man would take an interest in her while she was expecting someone else's child, but she decided to enjoy Harry's attention while it lasted. Whether it would lead anywhere was a question for another day. Either way, she'd be fine.

It had been more than a week since Kyla had left Earth-Song without a word. When Clay and Jennie helped her move out that quiet Friday night, the ecovillage had been deserted—most of the residents were away at a music festival on Hornby Island. Still, Kyla felt bad about leaving without saying goodbye to the friends she'd shared so much of her life with.

Today felt like the right day to make things right.

She stopped at The Sunrise Café to grab a coffee before heading over, and as she entered, Raine spotted her from across the room.

"Sundance!" Raine called out, rising from her seat. "Where have you been?"

Kyla mustered a smile and crossed the café. "Funny seeing you here," she said, trying to sound upbeat. "I was just on my way to EarthSong to say my goodbyes."

Raine took a sip of her coffee, eyeing Kyla over the rim of her mug. "We were wondering what happened to you. Figured maybe you moved off the island—or went back home."

"I left the night of the music festival," Kyla explained. "The place was deserted. I didn't get the chance to say goodbye."

"You could've left a note," Raine said with a hint of reproach. "But whatever—you're here now. So, what's going on?"

Before Kyla could answer, Raine's eyes suddenly lit up. "Oh! Guess what? Remember that guy who was working at EarthSong last November?"

Kyla's stomach dropped.

"He's back," Raine went on, completely unaware. "Been asking around for you. No one knew where you'd gone."

Kyla's mind raced. *Jude—back on the island?* She'd assumed she'd never see him again.

"Maybe you'll run into him today," Raine said, her tone casual. "He seemed kind of disappointed you weren't around."

"Maybe," Kyla said softly, her voice distant. "Thanks for telling me."

* * *

After parting ways with Raine, who headed across the street to the second-hand store, Kyla drove slowly away from the café. Once she was out of sight, she turned onto the first quiet side street and pulled over, parking away from any houses. Most people wouldn't recognize her in the SUV, she reasoned—after all, she was more often seen on her bicycle.

Kyla had given up hope of finding Jude again. She knew little about him other than that he had been the most captivating man she'd been with in years. It had been two-and-a-half months since they'd shared one unforgettable night, falling into each other's arms. By the time Kyla woke up the next morning, Jude was gone, catching the early ferry to the mainland. He was headed to Patagonia, with a stopover in Chile, and said he had a one-way ticket. Kyla never expected to see him again. She didn't even know where he lived, and there were no records kept in the ecovillage of the occasional workers who passed through. But, she thought, if he wanted to find her, he could.

"Did he come back to see me, specifically? Had he changed his mind about staying in Patagonia? Was he still at EarthSong, or had he left when no one knew where I'd gone? Kyla's mind buzzed with unanswered questions, each one deepening her confusion."

After parting ways, Kyla drove away from the café and turned onto a quiet side street, parking where no one would see her. She needed a moment. She hadn't expected to ever see Jude again after their one night together. He'd told her he was heading to Patagonia with a one-way ticket. She didn't even know his last name or where he lived—he had slipped out of her life as suddenly as he'd entered it. But now, he had come back. For her?

Kyla's thoughts spiraled. Could Jude be the father of her baby? And if he was, would she even want to be with him? The unanswered questions twisted inside her, intensifying her anxiety.

Sitting in her SUV, Kyla wrestled with the relentless 'what ifs. What if the baby grew up never knowing its father? What if that was her fault? The questions looped in her mind, leaving her more anxious with each passing minute.

She gripped the steering wheel, fed up with her indecision. Maybe Jude was still around. She had to find out.

Facing problems head-on wasn't Kyla's usual approach; she typically avoided them or tried to gloss over her concerns with optimism. But this time, she resolved to confront them directly. Otherwise, she knew she'd always wonder.

Chapter Thirty-Eight

Kyla felt a wave of nervousness as she pulled into the parking lot at EarthSong. She cut the engine and flipped down the visor mirror to check her reflection. *I have nothing to apologize for*, she reassured herself. *We're in this together.*

Her eyes scanned the ecovillage, hoping to catch sight of Jude. She kept a watchful eye as she stepped out of her vehicle and made her way up the stairs to the front entrance, where she noticed her friend Lily heading down.

"Lily," Kyla called out with a smile. The last time she'd spoken to Lily, who lived in one of the family units, Lily had congratulated Kyla on her "good news." That's when Kyla realized Raine hadn't kept her promise to keep Kyla's pregnancy a secret. But now, it didn't matter.

After a quick embrace, Kyla asked how things were going, and they exchanged brief pleasantries. Kyla was eager to reconnect with any of her friends still around, hoping to avoid the inevitable moment when she'd run into Jude. If that happened, she knew her chance to connect with the others would slip away.

As Kyla stepped into the lunchroom, the cacophony of conversations filled the air. Several people turned toward her, greeted her excitedly, and chatted with her about her unexpected return after a week and a half. Confidence radiated from her as she reciprocated their warmth, sparking easy conversations. She invited anyone interested to visit her at the farm.

With a final goodbye and a blown kiss to her friends, Kyla turned to exit the ecovillage—probably for the last time, she thought.

It wasn't until she opened the door of her SUV that she heard a deep male voice calling after her. She couldn't mistake that baritone. Kyla turned to see Jude walking swiftly across the gravel, kicking up small clouds of dust as he made his way toward her, seemingly in a hurry.

Jude pulled her into his strong arms, his embrace intense and passionate, sending a jolt through her. Her mind flashed back to that first night they'd shared, the one-night stand that had been over before the morning light. *There's a reason they call it a one-night stand*, she had reminded herself. *It's gone the next day.*

Jude's full lips met hers, pressing ever-so-softly before deepening the kiss, inviting her in. Kyla responded eagerly, letting her body betray how she felt about this man who had fathered her child. *It's impossible to make that kind of judgment on only our second meeting*, she told herself. *But at least this one's in the light of day.*

They pulled apart, laughing softly. "Guess we missed each other," Kyla said, hoping Jude felt the same connection she did.

"Why do you think I high-tailed it back from Patagonia before Christmas?" Jude asked, his blue eyes locked on hers.

"That says something, then, doesn't it, Jude?" A playful flirtation crept into Kyla's voice, replacing the nerves from earlier. "Hey, let me show you my new Forester, and we can grab some lunch and have an impromptu picnic at Ruckle Park if you're up for it."

"Cool," Jude replied with a mischievous look in his eye. "Lunch is on me," he added with a grin. "Just give me a minute. They've just laid out the lunch spread in the kitchen."

As Jude hastened back toward the main building, Kyla told him she'd find the perfect spot for their picnic.

The day was cloudy, with some sun peeking through—nothing like the perfect weather Kyla had shared with Harry on their hike up Mount Maxwell the day before. After considering a few options, she decided on Beddis Bay, hoping to catch some of the remaining morning light.

* * *

Kyla had no idea how she would tell Jude about the baby, but she trusted that the right moment would come. She tried to temper her excitement, though a small voice inside reminded her: *You don't know if he'll feel the same way.*

The beach at Beddis Bay was deserted when they arrived—perhaps a bit too early for a chilly December morning. Kyla was relieved, though, appreciating the privacy it offered, as much as one could expect in a public space. The white crushed shell beach stretched before them, gleaming in the morning sun. Kyla pointed out the tidal pools, which could be seen to their right at low tide.

Together, they spread out a waterproof picnic blanket from Kyla's hiking gear. Jude opened an insulated bag and pulled out turkey sandwiches, freshly made in the kitchen at EarthSong.

"That's my favorite of their lunchtime offerings," Kyla

remarked, feeling content in the unexpectedness of the moment with Jude. She took a bite of her sandwich, followed by a sip of the filtered water she'd packed in her backpack.

"So..." Jude began, his gaze lingering on Kyla as she kept her down winter jacket on, shielding herself from the chill offshore breeze. "Where did my ladylove disappear to? No one seemed to know where you'd gone. Is it your habit to vanish like Houdini without any warning?"

Kyla appreciated Jude's playful charm. His easygoing nature had drawn her in on that moonlit October night. She explained that she was ready for a change, and the most logical place to move, she said, was to her family's 1000-acre farm.

Jude raised an eyebrow. "Holee," he exclaimed. "A thousand acres? That's amazing. Is it an organic farm?"

"We're getting there," Kyla replied. "It takes a lot of work, as you know, but at least we've made a start."

Jude nodded thoughtfully. "Yes, but the idea of a completely 100% organic farm is just a myth."

"Oh, I know," Kyla said with a shrug. "Pesticides— dangerous ones—have been used for years, and it's impossible to wipe the slate clean just like that. Plus, our neighbors aren't organic, so residues from their operations inevitably cross over to Cliffhouse. But we do what we can, same as everyone else."

Jude paused for a moment, then asked, "I didn't even ask you, Kyla. Do you work outside of the ecovillage? Or, now that you're no longer living there, what do you do for a living? Can you support yourself working at Cliffhouse?"

Jude seemed particularly intrigued by Kyla's new setup, likely due to his interest in organic farming.

"I've been working at a veterinary clinic in Ganges for six years now," Kyla replied, her mind briefly drifting to Harry, and how only yesterday it had seemed like the beginning of a new chapter with him.

"Sounds like you've got it made, I must say," Jude responded, crumpling the sandwich wrapping and stowing it back in his bag.

As Kyla finished her lunch, she stood up and scooted off with the picnic blanket, motioning for Jude to join her as they walked toward the expansive sandy beach. The shallow water, a popular swimming spot in the summer, shimmered in the distance. The tidal pools, with their fascinating marine life, continued to captivate both kids and adults alike.

"The crushed-shell beach feels almost like a tropical paradise," Jude murmured, his eyes softening as he looked at Kyla. "Come closer, baby," he said, his voice low with desire. He drew her into his arms, enveloping her in a heated embrace. "I couldn't stop thinking about you, after that night in October."

He paused, his lips brushing hers in a kiss that deepened, leaving Kyla breathless and wanting more.

"I missed you, too, Jude," Kyla said softly, her voice betraying a hint of vulnerability. "But honestly, I didn't think I'd ever see you again." She paused, the excitement bubbling up within her, but she held it back, unsure of how to gauge his reaction. "I need to tell you something..." she added, hesitating. The last thing she wanted was for Jude to pretend everything was fine when it might not be.

"What is it, my love?" Jude asked, his term of endearment catching Kyla off guard. But she couldn't deny she liked it. There was something deeply satisfying about the father of her child expressing such warmth and passion for her.

Kyla slid her hands from Jude's shoulders to his hips, standing on her tiptoes to meet his gaze. His eyes—more vivid against the backdrop of the ocean—held her in a way that made her heart race. But then, just as quickly, she hesitated.

I'll tell him about the baby in the place where our child will grow up, maybe even be born, she thought. The moment felt too monumental to be rushed.

"Uh, on second thought," she said, her voice faltering slightly. "Why don't I show you the farm? You can see where I'm living now... and I know you'd enjoy Cliffhouse."

* * *

Kyla couldn't help but smile as Jude's gaze swept over the expansive property. They pulled up the long driveway, the early winter light casting a soft glow over the landscape. As they parked just outside her new home, Jude's reaction was immediate.

"This is amazing, Kyla," he said, his voice filled with admiration. He hopped out of the SUV, taking in the view as they walked across the breezeway. "Why stay at EarthSong when you could have lived here all along?"

Kyla paused for a moment, the quiet of the space enveloping them. "It's a long story," she said, keeping her tone light. "I spent four years in the ecovillage. Learned a lot. Made new friends. But it was time for a change, a new chapter," she added, sidestepping the deeper conversation that hovered on the tip of her tongue. She wasn't ready to share everything with him just yet.

The air inside Kyla's home was cool and refreshing, the scent of the ocean drifting in through the open windows, blending with the warmth of the room. She loved how the fresh sea breeze seemed to invigorate her spirit, and she often left the windows open, even in the colder months, just to keep that connection to the outside world.

"This way," Kyla said, her voice soft, guiding Jude toward the front door. She stopped for a moment, glancing around the room, feeling a subtle thrill of anticipation about showing him this part of her life.

"Welcome to my home," Kyla said with a playful, knowing smile, keeping her secret a little longer.

As she closed the door behind them, the sound of it shutting seemed to heighten the stillness of the space. Jude turned to face her, his eyes locking onto hers, filled with that familiar warmth and a growing intensity. Before Kyla could speak, he stepped toward her, his hands reaching out, pulling her close into a tight embrace. His lips found hers with an urgency that sent a surge of electricity through her. In that moment, everything else faded. All she could focus on was the heat of his kiss and the feeling of his arms around her.

For a brief second, Kyla let herself melt into him, forgetting everything but the way he made her feel.

When they finally pulled apart, Jude's gaze was intense, filled with unspoken questions. Kyla took a breath, steadying herself. She placed a hand on his chest, feeling the steady beat of his heart, and looked up at him with a nervous smile.

"There's something I need to tell you," she began, her voice trembling slightly but carrying the weight of the moment. "Jude, I'm pregnant."

Jude's expression shifted from surprise to something deeper, his eyes wide as he processed her words. He stepped back, as if physically recoiling from the revelation, and Kyla's heart skipped a beat. She immediately regretted how she'd said it—too blunt, too sudden.

"Pregnant?" he echoed, his voice hoarse.

Kyla nodded, her hands trembling slightly as she clasped them together in front of her. "Yes, Jude. I'm pregnant."

A long, heavy silence fell between them. Jude's expression was blank, as if his mind couldn't process what he'd heard. The quiet stretched out, thick with uncertainty, as if he was waiting for something more, some kind of explanation or reassurance that wasn't coming.

After what seemed like an eternity, Jude exhaled sharply and ran a hand through his hair. "I... I don't know what to say," he muttered, more to himself than to her.

Kyla felt her stomach flip. "You don't have to say anything, Jude. I just wanted you to know." Her voice softened, her heart racing as she waited for him to process everything.

Jude's eyes revealed a brief moment of something—regret, maybe, or uncertainty. He shook his head, as though trying to clear his thoughts, and then took a cautious step toward her. "But you don't know how this changes things, do you? I—" He stopped, his words trailing off, and his hands dropped to his sides.

"I know it changes things," Kyla said, her voice quiet but firm. "I wouldn't expect anything else."

She searched his face, hoping to find something to hold onto in the storm of emotions swirling in his eyes—perhaps a spark of hope that maybe this could work, despite everything.

Finally, Jude took both of her hands in his, looking past her shoulders at first, then fixing his gaze on Kyla. "Are you planning on keeping the baby, Kyla?"

Jude's question felt like an arrow piercing Kyla's heart. She pulled free of his hands, turning away. Tears streamed down her face as she felt the ultimate rejection of her pregnancy.

Jude reached for her. "Kyla, Kyla..." he pleaded. "Please, don't walk away. We need to talk."

Kyla turned to look at Jude. His demeanor spoke volumes, she thought. He didn't want to be a parent, and that realization was crushing. There was nothing he could say to make this better.

"Why didn't you use birth control?" Jude asked. To Kyla, it

felt as if their growing baby had been reduced to a mere technicality.

"We both know how it went," Kyla said, hurt. "What we're dealing with now," she said, pointing out the obvious, is an unwanted pregnancy." Fresh tears streamed down Kyla's reddened face.

Jude pulled her in close, attempting to soothe her grief. After a few moments, Kyla pulled away. They both looked up in surprise when Alexa shoved open the door and stood face-to-face with Jude.

"How dare you?" she screamed, sending shock waves through Kyla.

"How dare I what?" asked Jude.

"How dare you blame my sister for the pregnancy?"

"I wasn't blaming her," he said, his voice low but laced with tension. "I just asked—"

"Well, that's not how it came out," Alexa interrupted, her voice sharp with anger. She stood in the doorway, her hands clenched into fists at her sides. Her eyes were blazing with fury, worsened by Jude's attempt to twist the situation. "You don't get to do that. You don't get to come in here and make my sister feel like this is somehow her fault."

"When two people agree to make love, there's a dual responsibility, not a sole responsibility. But you, like all the other narcissists like you... "

Kyla wondered at that second if her sister was going to slam him. Yet, she did not attempt to stop Alexa. Instead, Kyla felt warmed by Alexa's response and proud of her sister for being there for her. At that moment, Kyla knew that she and Alexa were back.

Alexa turned to leave, but before stepping out the door, she added, "One thing I know for sure, Mr. Macho Man, you don't deserve my sister, the baby doesn't deserve to have a father like you, and you don't even begin to measure up to the standards followed by the Mitchell family for more years than you can probably even count."

Kyla watched as Alexa left the room, stomped across the driveway toward the orchards, and greeted Rollo like her long-lost buddy.

Feeling stronger now, Kyla figured out a few things right there and then. "I'm keeping the baby, Jude, and if you don't want to take responsibility, I won't fight you on it."

"I can't, Kyla; I just can't. Parenthood isn't in my vocabulary. I'm a traveller of the world, doing my best to help the planet, and the added responsibility of child-rearing, well, it just isn't part of my vision."

"You should have thought of that earlier," Kyla said. Fighting the urge to turn away, she paused, knowing she had someone other than herself to consider.

"Jude, I won't demand anything of you, except for whatever communication or visitation you can give. Just so my child has some connection, however slim, with her father. For my child's sake, I want to avoid a huge, trauma-filled wound that never heals.

"Understood, Kyla. I'll respect your wishes," Jude said. "I'm a father already, but I'm signing off as a traditional dad as of now, and I'm so sorry for all your distress."

There was nothing left to say, Kyla figured. "If you want a drive back to EarthSong, I'll drop you off."

As they snapped their seatbelts in Kyla's SUV, Kyla said to herself, "*My only distress is that you're here with me now.*" Her feelings of joy had been buried amidst feelings of sadness and despair. But now Kyla had something new to be grateful for—having her sister back.

* * *

In the parking lot at EarthSong, Jude stepped out of the passenger side and walked around to Kyla's open window on the driver's side. She stared straight ahead, unable to meet Jude's eyes—it hurt too much. But when he said goodbye, she listened closely.

"No matter where I am, Kyla, a part of you will always be with me."

In her mind, Kyla reconfigured his sentiment to align more with her reality. *No matter where I am, Jude, a part of you will always be with me.*

* * *

Steering the Forester back toward Cliffhouse, Kyla sighed heavily. *It's done; it's over,* she reassured herself, trying to stay positive. *I was happy without him, and I'll continue without him. I don't need Jude to validate my life or my baby's life. There was a chance, and I'm glad I took it—and now I know,* she thought as her tires crunched toward the stalwart family farm where she could rely on the people she loved—and that included Alexa.

Chapter Thirty-Nine

Kyla dragged herself through Monday morning, struggling to keep her focus at work. The exhaustion from the weekend clung to her like a shadow, making everything feel heavier. She couldn't match Harry's positive energy today.

As the workday wound down and the office emptied, Kyla shut down her computer while Harry lingered by her desk. She heard his soft voice say, "Hey," catching her just as she was about to leave. "You can't hide that hint of sadness in your eyes, no matter how hard you tried today."

Kyla stood up and instinctively rested her head against Harry's chest. He wrapped his arms around her, and for a moment, the rest of the world faded away. She knew Harry was probably worried someone might walk in, but he held her anyway, letting the quiet comfort of the moment linger despite the risk.

"I saw Jude yesterday, Kyla confided."

Leaning away from Kyla, Harry asked, "Who's Jude?"

"Oh, I'm sorry, Harry, I forgot you don't know that detail. And it's not important anyway."

Harry gently released Kyla, his warmth lingering even as he stepped away. She watched as he walked to the front door and turned the lock, a quiet gesture that told her it was okay to let her guard down, at least for a little while. She sank into a chair, feeling the weight of her grief pulling at her.

She poured out her troubles, and Harry listened, his eyes never leaving hers, his expression soft with understanding. When she finished, he paused, then said, "Not everyone can embrace parenthood, and maybe they should bow out early, for the sake of everyone involved."

Kyla nodded, taking in his words, though a subtle hesitation in his voice made her wonder what he wasn't saying. His jaw tensed, and something flickered in his eyes—judgment, maybe? She couldn't be sure. Whatever it was, he chose to keep it to himself. And for now, she was grateful for his presence, even if it didn't feel like the whole truth.

* * *

Kyla took a seat at the table, the rich aroma of Kathleen's famous lamb stew filling the air. With Jennie tied up in market preparations, Kathleen had stepped in, and Kyla felt a deep appreciation for the warm, home-cooked meal on a chilly December evening.

Kyla watched as Clay took his first bite, his eyes lighting up. "Kathleen, you're the best cook," he declared, grinning. "But don't tell your daughter that," he added with a wink, tossing a teasing glance in Jennie's direction.

Kathleen chuckled, clearly pleased, and offered Clay another helping. "I'm sure you burn a lot of energy running that paragliding school of yours," she said. "You need the extra fuel."

"All true," Clay said with a grin. "And Kathleen's Kitchen is the best restaurant in town."

Kyla smiled at their easy banter. It felt good to see everyone at ease, especially after how tense things had been lately.

Kyla usually cooked for herself at her place, but tonight, Kathleen had insisted she join them for her special dish. As dinner went on, Kyla felt her earlier weariness begin to fade. The warmth of the cozy kitchen, the easy laughter, and the comfort food seemed to fill her up in ways she hadn't realized she needed.

Kyla sensed Jennie watching her, as if she'd picked up on something different. Kyla shifted under her gaze, wondering what Jennie might have noticed.

"Kyla, I got you something today," Jennie said suddenly, her tone light but tinged with excitement. "How about we settle on the verandah? Clay's already got the heaters going, so it should be warm enough out there."

Kyla nodded, curious but also grateful for the distraction. She followed Jennie, trying to guess what her mother might have in mind.

"A gift for me, Mom?" Kyla asked, her eyebrows lifting in mock surprise. "You've already given me so many gifts over the years, my dearest mother in all the world..."

Jennie laughed, shaking her head, before reaching for a white paper gift bag from the dining room breakfront. "Just let me have my fun," she said with a wink.

Kathleen's cheerful, sing-song voice chimed in from the kitchen. "Want some tea, ladies?"

Kyla nodded, feeling wrapped in the gentle comfort of her family–a brief but welcome respite from the heaviness she carried.

The crisp December air nipped at Kyla's cheeks, even with the outdoor heaters radiating warmth. She gazed out across the flood-lit areas, the comfort of the verandah offering her peace. *I wonder if we'll get any snow this winter.* This place, these gatherings—they were some of the things she loved most about being back at Cliffhouse.

"If I had to choose only one thing as my favourite that our family does together here at Cliffhouse," Kyla said, glancing at Jennie, who had settled into one of the upholstered chairs, "it would resoundingly be our family gatherings on the verandah."

Jennie smiled at her, warm and knowing. Kyla knew her mother had heard this sentiment echoed by every family member in their own way over the years, but it still felt important to say.

"Here, dear, see what you think of this." Jennie handed her the white paper bag, the rustle of tissue paper filling the quiet space as Kyla carefully pulled out a hand-sewn baby romper. The intricate smocking on the bodice caught her eye, the tiny stitches so precise it felt like holding a piece of art.

"Mom, where did you find this?" Kyla asked, her delight evident.

"At the Christmas market, of course," Jennie said proudly. "Tammy Markham was setting up her stall, and I couldn't resist checking out the baby items."

"I love it, Mom," Kyla said, stepping forward to kiss Jennie's forehead. "So, you're excited about the baby?"

"I won't say I was anywhere near excited when I first heard the news," Jennie admitted, her voice softening. "But time goes by, doesn't it? And the more I thought about hearing the pitter-patter of another pair of Mitchell family feet, well—what is there not to look forward to?"

Kyla's heart warmed at her mother's words. "It makes my heart sing to hear that you feel that way, Mom. And, to tell you the truth, I'm becoming more and more excited as time goes by, too. I can't wait until I get the baby bump," she said, her tone a little shy as she glanced at Jennie.

"That'll come soon enough, Kye. Maybe by Christmastime," Jennie replied, her eyes soft with emotion.

Kyla hadn't yet told her mom about the complicated feelings she had for Harry, let alone the awkward meeting with Jude and his sudden departure. To Jennie, Jude was just a name that hadn't even come up, and Kyla was content to keep it that way, at least for now. She'd share things about Harry if they worked out, but for now, it was too soon to open up about it all.

Checking her phone, Kyla noticed it was already ten o'clock. She stood up, ready to head to bed, when Jennie caught her attention.

"Oh, before you go," Jennie said, "I wanted to let you know that Clay's son Patrick has confirmed his plans to come to Cliffhouse. He'll be here on the nineteenth, just in time to spend Christmas with us."

Kyla felt a mix of emotions at the news. Patrick's arrival stirred something uneasy in her, but she pushed the feeling down. *If this is what Clay and Jennie want, I'll do my best to support it. But why do I get edgy every time his name is mentioned?*

Patrick would be staying in the other unit of the side-by-side, away from her own space, but still, his presence loomed large in her mind. She had more pressing things to think about, like getting a good night's sleep.

"Oh, Clay will be excited to see Patrick, I'm sure," she said carefully. "I'll dust the place for him this weekend. If that side is anything like mine was, it won't take long until it's in move-in condition again."

"It'll be the same, Kye," Jennie said proudly. "I don't miss cleaning the units one bit, but I must say, I did keep everything sparkly clean when I did. And any dust collected over two years would only be from opening doors and windows occasionally to help air out the houses."

"You're a wonderful housekeeper, Mom," Kyla said, playfully adding, "Too bad you couldn't make an Irish stew like Grandma, though."

Jennie laughed, recalling Clay's playful teasing about her kitchen skills. "It's nice we can kid each other that way. Laughter truly is the best medicine."

Kyla lingered a moment longer, then remembered one last thing. "Now I have a 'by the way', Mom," she said, pausing on the verandah steps. "Do we know when Nick is coming home for Christmas?"

"We do," Jennie said, brightening. "He and Emily will arrive late next Friday night. I hope they'll make it to the Christmas market on Saturday, even for just a few minutes."

"It'll be so good to see Nick," Kyla said. "It's been far too long."

"I know," Jennie agreed. "When he and Emily took a stay-cation over the Spring Break, we didn't get to catch up like we usually do."

Kyla nodded thoughtfully. "This Emily person must be a big draw for him to miss celebrating Easter at the farm."

"Indeed," Jennie said with a smile. "We'll get the straight goods from Nick when the time seems right. Meanwhile, I look forward to meeting this woman who's captured your brother's heart."

Kyla watched Jennie's expression soften at the mention of Nick, and it struck her how much she missed those family gatherings when everyone was together. But for now, she tucked away her lingering questions and allowed herself to look forward to what was to come.

Chapter Forty

Saturday, December 17, had finally arrived, and Bev and Jennie were as ready as they could be. Bev had decorated the windows with wreaths and pine boughs, all natural, setting the tone for the theme of the annual Christmas market.

"Make it, grow it, or bake it" was the memorable mantra of the Sunrise Island Saturday Market, and that extended to the Christmas Indoor Market too. Handcrafted, homegrown, and homemade goods were the main draw for customers and sellers all over the island and beyond.

Jennie agreed with Bev's sentiment: "I think we need to expand our indoor market," she said amidst the hustle and bustle of the day.

"That's a great testament compared with when we started this almost twenty years ago," replied Jennie, bursting with pride. Glancing across the room at her watercolour nature paintings of Bodega Ridge on Galiano Island and Hope Bay on Pender Island, Jennie reflected on the joy of no longer being tied down to the B&B.

"Your large format landscape paintings are quite good, in my opinion," Bev remarked.

"Bev, thank you so much for drawing me to the world of painting. I love it. It's a great distraction from life's troubles and, you know, when I'm creating, I think of nothing else."

"Exactly," said Bev. "It was my saviour through my divorce and on through the decades. Highly recommended."

Jennie planned to keep an eye on the front entrance, hoping her son Nick and his girlfriend Emily would manage to make an appearance before the market closed. They had arrived only the night before. There was barely enough time for a welcome hug, an introduction to Emily, and information to help Emily settle in. Clay offered to drive them if they could be ready by 2:00 p.m., just one hour before closing. Alexa, Kyla, and Kathleen planned to leave in time to arrive for the opening at 10 a.m.

Offerings at the market included soaps, jewellery, art, clothing, woodwork, pottery, and musical instruments. In a separate area, cheeses, baked goods, preserves, fudge, spices, cider, wine, vinegars, kimchi, and even some lunch items were for sale.

Jennie noticed Bev at the front entrance, dealing with a customer who seemed upset. The man, in his fifties with thick grey hair, was arguing about the no-dogs policy.

"Oh, excuse me, sir," Bev said, her voice steady, "but dogs aren't permitted in the market. There's a doggie daycare just behind the building," she added with a friendly smile. "We have signs directing customers there."

The man, his pit bull mix tightly leashed, looked taken aback. "What? This is Sunrise Island, the land of hippies and do-as-you-will, right?" he retorted, his irritation evident. "I ate at a pub last night where dogs were welcome. I assumed it'd be the same here."

Bev remained unflappable, her red hair bright against her calm demeanor. "Yes, this is Sunrise Island, but we have regulations for everyone's safety," she explained. She then stepped toward the open door, gesturing for him to follow so she could show him the daycare.

The man followed reluctantly, mumbling, "Okay, lady, I see where the so-called daycare is. No need to daycare me," his tone dripping with annoyance.

Bev maintained her courtesy, saying, "Thank you. You're welcome inside whenever you're ready," before turning back into the building, her frown barely hidden.

"What was that all about?" asked Jennie, immediately noticing Bev's changed demeanor.

"What an a-hole," she said, uncharacteristically. "Belligerent because I asked him to put his dog in the daycare. It's clearly marked." Bev shook her head, letting off some steam.

"There's always one, isn't there, Bev?" Jennie said, her voice low as she glanced at the lingering customer who'd been causing trouble.

Jennie caught the unwavering determination in Bev's eyes, knowing she wasn't one to let anything dampen her spirits.

"But I won't let this guy ruin the huge success we're seeing here today," Bev said with a confident smile, her gaze sweeping across the bustling room filled with excited shoppers checking prices and eagerly planning their holiday gifts. The scene was a testament to all their hard work, and Jennie could see Bev was soaking it all in, savouring the moment.

Just so you know, Mom, Alexa, and Kyla are here," Jennie said, noticing Bev's eyes light up with delight as she scanned the room. "They arrived while you were handling that man and his dog."

Bev wasted no time making her way to Jennie's daughters,

her two favourites. She enveloped each in a warm hug. Jennie observed with a knowing smile as Bev gave Kyla a longer embrace. Jennie had finally shared the news of Kyla's pregnancy with her best friend. Now, everyone knew except Nick.

Jennie watched as Bev's face brightened at the sight of Alexa and Kyla. It had been almost a month since Bev had last seen them, and the news of their reconciliation thrilled her. "And where's your grandmother?" Bev asked, clearly delighted to have them all together again.

"Grandma's chatting with Stewart Owen," Kyla giggled. "We always hoped they'd be together," she confided, her laughter infectious.

Jennie enjoyed seeing Bev laugh, her eyes crinkling with amusement. "Ah, I think your mother used to buy organic bacon for her B&B from Stewart's farm," Bev said. "He and Kathleen are true community treasures," she said, glancing at Kathleen and Stewart, who were engrossed in conversation, completely unaware of the bustling crowd around them. Jennie followed Bev's gaze, noting the comfortable familiarity between the two. "But you know how it is—opposites attract, and they're not opposites," Bev mused, her voice tinged with a hint of wistfulness. Jennie nodded, sharing a warm sense of camaraderie with Bev as they exchanged this quiet observation.

Jennie followed Alexa's gaze to Kathleen and Stewart. She observed how Stewart nodded thoughtfully at Kathleen's words while Kathleen, as always, was deeply engaged in their conversation. Jennie admired how Kathleen, even in her later years, remained direct and dedicated to everything she took on. From Jennie's vantage point, it looked like they'd been talking nonstop for about ten minutes.

Jennie watched Kyla, absorbed in her own world as if the bustling market had faded away. Kyla picked up a handcrafted pottery mug, her fingers gently tracing the three-toned glaze over its textured surface. She seemed completely captivated by the technique.

Jennie overheard Bev's gentle question, "Do you think you'll ever get back to making pottery, Kyla?"

Kyla's eyes lit up with enthusiasm. "Well, you know, Auntie Bev, I was just thinking about that. Now that I'm back at Cliffhouse, I might dust off Mom's pottery wheel and give it a try again. We'll see."

Jennie felt a warm sense of contentment. It was heartening to see her daughters so engaged and to be surrounded by family and friends, all sharing in the joys of the season.

* * *

By lunchtime, Alexa, Kyla, and Kathleen left the market. Alexa noticed Kyla's satisfaction with her new wood pepper mill, something Kyla couldn't make herself.

Alexa herself had bought a selection of handmade soaps. The earthy fragrance of the bars filled the car on the drive back home, a pleasant reminder of their market visit. She glanced at Kyla, who was sitting in the passenger seat, and saw her smiling knowingly at Kathleen in the back seat.

Kathleen had met up with Stewart at the market and seemed happy. Alexa listened as Kathleen remarked, "You know, that Stewart Owen is a fine man. I always thought so. We've known each other for a lifetime."

Alexa smiled as Kyla turned to Kathleen and said, "You know, Grandma, you two would make a fine pair."

Kathleen burst out laughing, and Alexa could hear the amusement in her voice. "I think you two have tried to match-make Stewart and me for years," Kathleen said, leaning forward so Alexa could hear too. "But there's every kind of relationship these days, and I can tell you that both of us are just fine with the way things stand between us. Have been for years. So, thanks very much for the encouragement, ladies, but it's entirely unnecessary." Alexa noticed the faraway look in Kathleen's eyes and the pleased smile on her face.

Chapter Forty-One

Jennie paused to admire a flower vase displayed in Mira's stall. Picking it up and turning it toward the light, she reveled at the luminescent glow of the crystalline glaze on porcelain. "This is my favourite piece, Mira. I just might have to purchase it from you. I've never worked with a glaze like that, although it always draws my eye."

"Shall I save it for you, Jen?" Mira offered, ready to move it behind her table so no one else could purchase the one-of-a-kind piece.

"Oh, no," Jennie replied. "I'm just going to get a bite to eat, and then I'll be back. The smells coming from that food table are driving me wild."

They'd positioned the food stalls on each side of the entryway as a further enticement to passersby. Scents of organic chicken sandwiches, homemade sausages and salami, oven-fired pizza, and falafel burgers wafted across the room. With only two hours to closing, Jennie's stomach rumbled, and the energy expended to get this far in the day's activities was taking a toll.

As she headed toward the food stall, her mouth watering with the thought of a housemade turkey-and-cranberry sausage on a sesame seed bun, she recognized Mrs. Logan, an elderly woman with visual impairment, making her way up the steps with her standard poodle held by a sequined pink leash.

Jennie saw that Bev was on the case. After some conversation, Mrs. Logan proceeded into the room with her seemingly well-behaved, black poodle.

"Misty is a guide dog, as you know, so they're allowed to come in," Bev advised Jennie.

"Okay," said Jennie. "Mrs. Logan seems to go everywhere with Misty, so I guess she knows what she's doing. But don't you think it odd that she'd attempt to navigate a crowded spot such as this?"

"I do indeed," agreed Bev, "but she's on a mission. She told me that she's here for one thing: Lady Rose Relish."

"Ah," replied Jennie, smiling. "She'll have to keep that doggie close in this crowd." Bev's eyes swept the hall. "There are two stalls that might carry that relish. I could have enquired on her behalf," suggested Bev, realizing that her rumbling tummy had gotten the better of her judgment. Besides, she had witnessed Mrs. Logan navigate tight quarters with Misty many times, and she was a regular at the outdoor market.

"She's moving slowly," observed Jennie. "She seems to be headed in the right direction," Bev remarked, as Mrs. Logan paused to speak to one of the stall attendants.

"Hey," Bev said, apparently no longer concerned about Misty and Mrs. Logan, "that bacon-and-cheese burger is calling my name."

As the two enjoyed their lunch, they chatted about how smoothly things were going. "Sure is," Jennie agreed, "You can sense the joy in the room. You know, just like us, I think people are happy to be out doing what they used to do before the pandemic."

Having taken a big bite of her tasty burger, Bev nodded vigorously.

"Hey Mom," Nick interjected as he approached her and Bev at the food stall.

"Nick, you made it." Jennie gave her son a quick hug. Then she warmly greeted Nick's girlfriend, meeting her for the first time. "Welcome, Emily. I was hoping you'd visit the market while you're here. It's only one day, but as you can see, a popular day."

Emily smiled, her long blond hair in perfectly constructed French braids. Glancing over the room full of shoppers, Emily returned her attention to the food stalls where Jennie and Bev were having their lunch. "Smells good in here," she remarked.

Jennie watched as Nick greeted Bev with an enthusiastic hug. "Auntie Bev, so good to see you. And I don't think you've met my girlfriend, Emily," he said, his voice full of warmth.

Jennie smiled as Bev turned to Emily with a welcoming expression. "Pleased to meet you, Emily. If you want to get a sense of island culture, this is a good place to be," Bev said proudly, her eyes sparkling with pride.

Just then, Clay entered the hall, his eyes immediately finding Jennie just finishing her lunch.

"Clay," Jennie beckoned, "you must try this." She handed the last of her bun to Clay, who made short work of the last tasty fragment.

Before Clay could comment, Jennie watched as a motley-coated pit bull cross darted into the hall off-leash with no owner in sight. Spotting Mrs. Logan's guide dog still held on a leash by her elderly owner, the pit bull charged toward the dog, growling. He nipped poor, hapless Misty on her back, causing her to bark and snap at the bully. Misty pulled so hard on the leash, she broke free of her owner's hand, giving chase to the pit bull.

Slamming into the leg of Mira's display table, the whole thing came crashing to the ground. Onlookers screamed, a toddler was knocked over as the pit bull bumped into him, and the pristine white floor was marred with muddy footprints.

In the chaos, the dogs stepped on the edges of long white linen tablecloths, causing more handcrafted merchandise to smash to the floor. Jennie watched in horror as her favourite crystalline vase broke in two.

She saw Clay hurry to the scene as best he could. The crowd had largely dispersed, some exiting promptly while others lined the walls, uncertain of what to do. As parents lifted young ones into the safety of their arms, Clay made several attempts to grab Misty's leash, and when finally successful, he returned the dog to Mrs. Logan and asked Nick to help her exit safely.

Jennie and Bev watched in disbelief. The scene before them seemed so alien that they sat in suspended animation as Clay and others tried to redirect the pit bull outside.

Jennie's attention was abruptly drawn to a booming voice near the front entrance. She turned to see the belligerent man with the thick grey hair from earlier. He commanded his dog to come, his voice harsh and impatient. Jennie watched as the man threw folded-up paper money onto the glass deli case, his impatience evident.

Snapping the leash onto his dog's collar, he fed it a piece of beef without a hint of apology or concern for the chaos surrounding him. His blatant disregard for the decorum of the place and its people left Jennie seething.

He quickly exited, tramping down the steps without glancing back toward the hall.

Bev and Jennie, with Clay following closely, followed the man to his car, parked across the road in Grace Square.

Jennie heard Bev shout, "Just a moment. You can't leave," she demanded, incredulous at the man's audacity.

"Watch me," he said, raising the trunk of his car and commanding his dog to get inside. He removed the leash and slammed the door shut, turning to glare at his followers. "If you think that you can leave your front door open with the smell of meat filling the air and not expect it to attract animals, well, you need to give your head a shake," he yelled.

Jennie felt proud when Clay stood up to the stranger. "Now, look," Clay intercepted before the man could open the front door of his SUV, "you've caused a lot of damage here today. It's a wonder no one was seriously hurt."

As Clay tried to reason with the man, Bev took several pictures of his license plate, vehicle, and of the man himself."

Glancing over Clay's shoulder, the man shouted to Bev, "Lady, you don't have permission to take my picture. Give me that phone."

Jennie was appalled to see the man lurch toward Bev. Clay stretched out his foot, causing the man to face-plant on the hard asphalt. He cried out in pain and lay on the hard parking lot floor for a moment before attempting to get up.

Jennie noticed the crowd that had gathered behind. Such a scene was highly uncommon on Sunrise Island, and people looked shocked at the scene before them. As Clay attempted to help the man to his feet, the man shoved him away, blood streaming down his face.

Jennie studied the man as he pressed a hand against his nose, started his vehicle, stepped harder on the gas pedal than was appropriate in a public space, and drove forward out of his parking space. Everyone watched as he screeched out of the parking lot heading south.

A mixture of anger, disbelief, and sadness showed on the faces of Jennie, Bev, and Nick. Nick hugged his mother, "Sorry, Mom, you two didn't deserve that."

Jennie saw streaks of blood on Clay's left shirt sleeve. "I'll call Ben," he said to Jennie, hoping to ease her mind.

"I already did," Jennie said, confident that the local RCMP officer, a long-time friend, would get right on the case.

Jennie wasn't surprised to hear Bev move forward as she showed her characteristic 'get'er-done' attitude. "We have a big mess to clean up, folks, so let's get started."

As they reached the stairs at the hall entrance, they were greeted with hugs from islanders who said they were there to help clean up.

"Em and I can help clean up, too, Mom," offered Nick, but Jennie refused.

"No," she said, "you and Emily and Clay just go home. The crafters will clean up their stalls, and these lovely people have also kindly offered to help. Bev and I will close the market early with a note of apology on the front door, and oversee the end of what was a highly successful event." Jennie tried to put a positive spin on what had just happened, but she couldn't deny a measure of sadness that it ended this way.

Bev pitched in. "We'll apologize to those who lost revenue because of this buffoon, and hope to collect insurance for the breakages." Then, addressing the half dozen volunteers who'd come to assist, she said, "You guys are the best. Typical islanders who show up when they're most needed and without hesitation. We can't thank you enough."

"It's the island way, isn't it?" one of the volunteers asked without expecting an answer. "And, hey, 'tis the Christmas season, too," she added, heading up the steps resolutely, while the others followed.

* * *

As they locked the market hall, concluding another year of the Sunrise Island Christmas Market, Jennie sensed that Bev had something to say. "You know that craft distillery over on Toynabee Road?" Bev asked. And then, without waiting for an answer, she added, "I think there's a bottle of premium spirits over there with our name on it."

Playing along, Jennie grinned, adding, "Yeah," and I hear the place is dog-friendly, so we may find our favourite buffoon in the tasting room."

"That'd be his unlucky day, don't you think?" asked Bev, laughing.

"Oh, it's always good to laugh, my friend," Jennie said, "But you know, at the end of the day, the market was still a huge success."

The camaraderie between old friends continued as Jennie watched Bev step into her car, smiling sweetly. "It was a huge success, Jen. But, next year, let's keep the front door shut."

Chapter Forty-Two

Kathleen's heart warmed the moment she heard Nick's incredulous voice echo from the stairwell.

"You didn't, Grandma." His eyes were wide as he and Emily clomped down the wooden stairs, finally making their way into the kitchen. Kathleen watched as Nick flung open the fridge door, his face lighting up like a child who'd just discovered sprinkles on his ice cream cone. There it was: his grandmother's famous satiny white angel food cake, proudly displayed on the old glass pedestal that had been in the family for as long as she could remember. A family favourite now, but Kathleen remembered when she'd first baked it for Nick's sixth birthday. She still chuckled at the memory of the cheeky finger-swipe he'd done that day, and she wondered now if he wasn't tempted to do it again. To Kathleen, that cake wasn't just dessert; it was part of Nick's legacy. And, she mused, long after she was gone, her angel food cake would still be known as Grandma's angel food.

"Food for the angels, Nick," Kathleen teased, enjoying the way his grin seemed to grow even wider. As she turned her attention to Emily, she offered a welcoming smile. "Coffee's made, dear, so please help yourself."

Nick shut the fridge door, a carton of almond milk in his hand. Kathleen could see the contentment in his eyes, the kind that made her feel she'd done something right. She gestured to the stove. "Care for some apple pancakes?" she asked, directing the offer to both of them.

"Grandma is an absolute treasure, Em," Nick said, his tone brimming with pride. Kathleen's heart skipped a beat at the words, though she couldn't help but notice that he had yet to introduce Emily properly.

But Emily stepped forward, extending her hand with a warm smile. "Oh, I know who you are, Kathleen. I'm very pleased to meet you and, I have to say, I feel as if I know you already. Nick has told so many stories about you."

Kathleen's chest swelled, pride radiating through her as she tried to process that Nick had been sharing tales of their times together. She never would have guessed he talked about her so much, especially to someone as important as Emily.

Nick wrapped his arm around Kathleen's shoulders, pulling her in close. "Best grandma anyone could ever have," he said, placing a quick kiss on her cheek. Kathleen couldn't help but smile, a deep, satisfied joy settling in as Nick released her.

"And another thing, Em," Nick added, his voice filled with boyish excitement. "Grandma's apple pancakes are to die for."

Kathleen's smile lingered, her heart brimming with contentment. There was something undeniably special about being seen this way through Nick's eyes—cherished, beloved, and a little bit legendary.

* * *

Comfortable and happy in her half of the side-by-side, Kyla let the familiar comfort of Cliffhouse wrap around her like a warm blanket. Yesterday morning's walk across the breezeway to the clifftop still clung to her, filling her with a carefree lightness she hadn't felt in far too long. As she set out again this morning, Rollo darted toward her with boundless energy, his wagging tail a blur of joy as he joined her, his exuberance echoing her own.

She made her way across the field, the soft crunch of the grass underfoot grounding her in the present. As she reached the edge of the cliff, she spotted Clay gliding gracefully past in his paragliding gear, a streak of vibrant colour against the blue sky. Kyla waved, a swell of gratitude blooming in her chest for her mother and Clay. They were happy, and in this place, with these people, she was too.

Kyla's thoughts drifted to Jude—his name more of a shadow than a presence now. She wondered if she'd ever see him again, but the question felt less important than it once was. *My happiness does not depend on Jude...or on any man*, she reminded herself firmly. *I don't need a man to validate me or anything about my life.* These strong convictions made her think of her Grandmother Kathleen, a role model whose wisdom had prepared her for so many of life's twists and turns. She hoped to be that kind of guide for her own child someday, but she knew she had to navigate her rough patches first.

Standing there, with the wind whipping around her and the sea stretching out endlessly before her, Kyla knew that her happiness was here. It was in the family that had stood by her, in the land that had been theirs for generations, and in the new life she would soon bring into the world. Seven months from now, she would have her contribution to the Mitchell family legacy, a thought that both thrilled and steadied her.

As for Dr. Harry Nicholls, only time would tell if anything meaningful develops between them. But back at Cliffhouse,

Kyla felt more confident than ever that she could face whatever the future may hold, whether or not a man is by her side. The prospect didn't scare her—it empowered her. Right now, she was content. She looked forward to Christmas at Cliffhouse, the annual tradition she and Alexa had cherished since they were kids.

"Kye!" Alexa's voice carried across the field, pulling Kyla from her thoughts. Kyla turned to see her sister hurrying toward her, her coat zipped tight against the chill. "Let me catch up," Alexa called, her cheeks flushed from the cold.

"Brrr, it's getting cold out, isn't it?" Alexa said as she reached Kyla, shivering slightly.

"Well, it is December, my dear," Kyla teased, her smile broadening at the sight of her sister. Alexa's unexpected arrival was a welcome surprise. "But let's head back. The outdoor heaters are on for Grandma, and I'm sure she'd love some company on the verandah. Are you joining us for Sunday dinner?"

"I am," Alexa replied, her voice sing-song and noticeably cheerful.

Kyla raised an eyebrow, catching the contagious joy radiating off her twin. "And what brings that gigantic smile to your face this crisp December afternoon, may I ask?" She nudged Alexa playfully, eager to unravel the source of her delight.

Alexa laughed, a bright sound that lifted the air around them. "Ha, I can't slip too much past you, can I?"

"Correct," Kyla said, grinning. "Now, what has happened?"

"Dr. Kevin Hunter, that's what has happened," Alexa announced joyfully, her eyes sparkling. "He asked me out. After all this time."

Kyla's eyes widened. "Ooh, Lexi, that is juicy news, indeed. I want to hear all about it. Tonight. After dinner. You and I in our old bedroom trading secrets, just like the old days."

As they walked back toward Cliffhouse, Kyla felt a deep sense of belonging. The walls of their home held so many secrets—moments of laughter, tears, and the unbreakable bond between sisters. And in that quiet, reflective moment, Kyla realized that even with all her past mistakes, she was truly blessed. This was her legacy, her family, and she was ready for whatever came next.

* * *

Thank you so much for reading *Sunrise Island Sisters*. Are you ready for Book Three in the *Sunrise Island Series?*

Immerse yourself in the festive spirit as the Mitchell family gathers together for a season brimming with love, laughter, and the joy of being home.

Rediscover the power of family bonds and the magic of holiday surprises in this heartwarming continuation of the family saga. Don't miss out—order your copy of ***Sunrise Island Christmas*** today!

* * *

Did you see the **FREE RECIPE** for Kathleen's glorious angel food cake? They don't call it "angel food" for nothing...

Bonus Recipe

A Taste of the Mitchell Family's Holiday Magic

In the Mitchell family, food isn't just a meal—it's tradition, memories, and a way to bring everyone together.

Now, you can bring a piece of that magic into your own home with this special recipe from Kathleen's Kitchen. Happy baking!

Kathleen's Angel Food Cake

Enjoy Kathleen's Angel Food Cake with your loved ones like the Mitchell family does every holiday season!

Ingredients:
- 1 ½ cups egg whites (10-12 large eggs)
- 3/4 cup flour
- ¼ cup cornstarch
- 1 ½ cups granulated sugar, divided
- ½ teaspoon salt
- 1 ¼ teaspoons cream of tartar
- ½ teaspoon vanilla extract

Instructions:

1. Preheat the Oven: Set your oven to 350°F (175°C). Make sure the oven rack is in the lowest position.

2. Sift the Flour, Cornstarch, and half the Sugar (¾ cup) together, 3 times: Set aside.

3. Beat the Egg Whites: Place egg whites in a large mixing bowl and sprinkle the salt and cream of tartar over the surface. Beat egg whites until stiff but not dry, gradually beat in remaining sugar and vanilla, and continue beating until the mixture forms stiff peaks but is not dry.

4. Fold in the Flour Mixture: Fold in gently, 2 tablespoons at a time.

5. Pour and Bake: Gently pour the batter into an ungreased 10-inch tube pan. Bake for approx 30 minutes, or until the top is lightly browned and the cake springs back when lightly touched with fingertips.

6. Cool and Serve: Invert tube pan on the neck of a large bottle (insert the neck of the bottle into the hollow tube) and let the cake cool completely. Once cooled, run a knife around the edges to release the cake from the pan.

But wait! How about that glossy, white frosting that Nick can't help but finger-swipe every chance he gets?

Fluffy White Frosting

Combine in saucepan:
    1 cup sugar
    1/3 cup water
    dash of salt
    1/4 tsp cream of tartar

Bring to boil, stirring until sugar dissolves

Very slowly add sugar syrup to 2 unbeaten egg whites in

mixing bowl, beating constantly with electric mixer until stiff peaks form (7 min. or longer)

Beat in 1 tsp vanilla

Frost top and sides of angel food cake

No finger swiping!

About the Author

Maren Hill

Captivated by the intrigue of everyday life, Maren Hill writes heartfelt, emotional stories that celebrate women and the relationships that shape their lives.

Quirky, good-hearted characters you'd love to know, and stories laced with romance, humour, compassion, and inspiration are trademarks of Maren Hill's books.

J.D. Monk

Written by children's book author JD Monk, *Slimy Slick* appeals to both children and adults with fascinating facts about banana slugs.

If you enjoy my books, please leave a review. There's nothing more motivational than positive reviews. Thank you so much.

Also by Maren Hill

Cliffhouse Footprints

Cliffhouse by the Sea

Sunrise Island Sisters

Sunrise Island Christmas

Sunrise Island Celebrations

Nicole

The Troublemakers

Our Forever Place

Make a Spectacular Seashell Lamp

Sealed with a Kiss

What Readers Say

Maren Hill's description of the island is so real that you can smell the salt air, feel the sand between your toes, the sun sparkling on the water, and hear the waves. Maren Hill weaves her stories extremely well.

... she has a real knack for transporting the reader to the world of the story.

The characters are great and the story is ... captivating.

Awesome. Great setting, and relatable characters with solid backgrounds. Well written... character portrayal is solid with depth.

... a suspenseful and mysterious story... will keep you on the edge of your seat.

Excellent knack for transporting the reader into the world of the story... I can't wait for more. A true gem!

I thoroughly enjoyed ... Cliffhouse by the Sea... kept me wanting to know what would happen next.

Maren Hill has done it again! Love this book. Would definitely read more by her.

This story with Alexa and Kyla was riveting. I really enjoyed the dynamics of these two sisters. This is a great story.

Beautifully done and exceptionally entertaining, heart-wrenching and delightful.

Gorgeous writing! I love the author's rich descriptions of characters, scenes and situations - I felt like I was living it.

* * *

JD Monk writes with a simplicity that pulls kids into the story immediately, but also with an underlying complexity and intelligence that allows the ideas in Slimy Slick to stay with them long after the tale ends. Well done!

This is a great story. Congratulations to the author for bringing awareness to these little creatures who are often misunderstood and undervalued. I love the education/entertainment combo. The illustrations are engaging and hilarious.

Beautifully written and illustrated -- this is a wonderful bedtime story! Not only do we learn about the importance of banana slugs in our ecosystem in this story, but we're introduced to lovely language to increase the richness of our vocabulary. This is an awesome gift for children (and their parents) who are curious about their environment!

What a wonderful read! It was extremely informative about Banana Slugs; a very misunderstood creature. I learned a lot! The graphics are very well done! Definitely a must buy this Holiday Season for the little ones in the family!

Loved this book! Very well written, easy to understand and follow for children! Super informative as well, I had no idea slugs were this unique!

I have a whole new appreciation for slugs...The kids love it.

... full of amazing facts about slugs... Completely recommend for curious kids who love nature.

The fun facts were marvelous and very informative. 5 stars to the author. Highly recommend.

Great book, full of lots of interesting slug facts. I recommend this for all young and young-at-heart bug lovers.

Perfect for storytime and a wonderful way to explore nature!

SLIMY SLICK—Not Just for Kids

The Nighttime Adventures of a Banana Slug

This captivating picture book appeals to kids and adults through multiple reads and is jam-packed with suspense, slime, and fun facts.

Join Slimy Slick on his exciting nighttime adventure through the countryside as he glides toward the tasty treat of his dreams. He encounters an earthworm and a shrew, but the real danger lies ahead. Will Slick's journey come to an abrupt end at the hands of a well-meaning boy whose mission is to capture and eliminate? Does he not understand Slick's important role in the ecosystem?

Readers learn about the clever design of the banana slug and how Slick uses his natural gifts to protect himself and navigate life in the wild.

Discover the world of Slimy Slick through a rainforest adventure that educates and entertains, emphasizing the importance of these fascinating creatures to our planet.

Perfect for:

• Parents and grandparents, science teachers, librarians, educators

• Gifts for kids who love nature, rainforest animals, and learning more about the natural world and zoology

• Read-aloud family sharing

• Gaining environmental wisdom

• Understanding empathy and collaboration

Acknowledgments

To my three daughters, who embody the true essence of sisterhood. Your unwavering love and support for each other have been a constant source of inspiration. Watching you grow together, laugh together, and lift each other up has shown me the beauty and strength of sisterly love—something I've tried to capture in *Sunrise Island Sisters*.

Special thanks to readers Jane Litherland and Terri Morgans for their keen insights and for finding what I missed.